Clarisse

Clarisse

an honest woman

Patricia Borlenghi

Patrician Press ● Manningtree

Patricia Borlenghi has an MA in Creative Writing. She lives in East Anglia and enjoys travelling. *Clarisse* is her first contemporary novel.

'*There is a powerful allusion here to one of the fundamental archetypes of the European novel, but with several twists. Borlenghi's Clarisse might be an "honest woman" (almost) like Richardson's "redeeming virgin", but she is Clarisse not Clarissa, indeed "Clarisse in Potignac". Clarisse might be in Potignac but she is not really French, or really English for that matter. She is in a sense Italian, at least in part.*
Clarisse's great-grandmother, whose story she is writing "in the form of a novel", was of Italian descent. Her name was Raiza, a transparent anagram of Zaira, who is the protagonist of Patricia Borlenghi's first novel.
 Watch out for this and other refined narrative ruses in a novel which races through like a thriller while engaging with the great issues of life' Verina Jones

Published by Patrician Press 2013.
New edition published by Patrician press 2015.
For more information: www.patricianpress.com.

First published as an e-book by Patrician Press 2013
This new revised edition published by Patrician Press 2015
Copyright © Patricia Borlenghi 2015

The right of Patricia Borlenghi to be identified as the
author of this work has been asserted in accordance with
the Copyright, Designs and Patents Act of 1988.

British Library Cataloguing in Publication Data. A catalogue
record for this book is available from the British Library.

ISBN 978-0-9930106-6-8

Printed in Peterborough by Printondemand-worldwide

www.patricianpress.com

For C. J.

Many thanks to Malcolm Dean for his information on New Zealand level crossings and to him and Andrew Goulden for their information about Auckland.

Many thanks also to Sandra Kramer, Karen Dixey, Tim Roberts, Jan Turner, Lynn Inglis, Joceline Bury, Claire Jakens, Andrea Borlenghi, Dr Phil Terry and, of course, to Charlie Johnson.

Thanks to Tim Roberts for his "Magnox (Pattern Paper)" lino-cut print for the cover illustration.

"Les morts dansaient et la longue file de squelettes tournait et tourbillonnait en une immense spirale, qui montait jusqu'aux hauteurs les plus hautes et descendait jusqu'aux abimes les plus profonds."
Gustave Flaubert. *La Danse des Morts*. 1838.

The Visit

Me. Who is Me?
Who am I?
When I look in the mirror
Who do I see? My parents made me,
God did not make me in his own image.
God did not make me to know him,
Love him and serve him in this world
And be happy with him forever in the next.
My parents made me.
They donated their genes.
I can only be me.
When I die that will be the end.
Dieu n'existe pas pour moi.
And I will remember this day.

Clarisse looked at herself in the mirror often, searching her skin for blemishes but also searching for her soul, her inner being, the meaning of her life.

When I look in the mirror, I see nothing there – a shadowy face with lots of dark, curly unmanageable hair and fuzzy features. I am totally unhappy. Nothing ever happens. I am bored. Reading is the only thing I enjoy. My parents say I am too young to have a boyfriend but I never meet any boys anyway. And if I do, I can't think what to say and then mumble something completely weird. I wish I could grow up. Be less shy, stop going red all the time. I must learn how to do this. Practise being smiley and confident… Pretend I'm Helen of Troy, except she didn't really exist, although I like to think she did… Homer created her. Paris seduced her. She's a character from the Iliad, part of Greek mythology but some people, somewhere might still believe in Greek or Roman gods and goddesses. Why not? It's okay to believe in a Christian God, Jesus Christ and the Holy Ghost (and believe in ghosts) and all that but not Zeus or Hera, Jupiter or Juno and all the other gods and goddesses... I wish they did exist. It would be fun to live in Olympus and look down on the mere mortals... playing with them, changing them into swans, stags, snakes...

*

She had a bad cold, or even 'flu. When she woke up that morning in her London home, she felt hot and clammy. Delphine, her mother, was worried and said:

'Darling, you're hot! You must go to the doctor.'

'Mum, I love you worrying about me but I don't need a doctor!'

Clarisse didn't like talking to doctors. Her symptoms always seemed to disappear as soon as she walked inside the surgery.

Delphine thought doctors should be respected and revered. It was a very good profession: 'Darling, you could be a doctor! Why don't you study medicine when you go to university?'

'No, Mum!' Clarisse laughed fondly. Her mother was very ambitious for her but Clarisse hated blood and diseases. She really didn't want to see a doctor but her mother insisted. 'You have a high temperature, darling. It's best that you go after school.'

To keep her mother happy, Clarisse relented.

'Okay, let's do it...' Clarisse hugged her mum and kissed her warmly on both cheeks.

Delphine had an appointment that evening for her blood-pressure check so she took Clarisse with her. It was just up the road from their house. They walked there arm in arm.

Clarisse took a deep breath but exhaled quickly as they entered the surgery waiting room. Ever since she was a small child, Clarisse had detested that pervasive disinfectant smell and the worn linoleum floor, immaculately scrubbed and polished. She remembered the surgery itself containing tall glass cabinets arrayed with assorted brown bottles of syrups or tinctures and tubs of greasy ointment. A few antique leather chairs were scattered around a stately mahogany desk, which was set at an angle in the centre of the room, cluttered with ink bottles; squeamish-green and sick-yellow pungent tonics or lurid purple and plum-red over-sweet cough mixtures and small white boxes of tablets, waiting for patients' names to be inscribed on their labels; piles of virgin prescription pads, newspapers, journals and magazines; its semi-open multiple-sized drawers brimming over with documents, forms, leaflets, pens, paper clips…

In the old days, there had been three old gentlemen in attendance, a Doctor O'Shea and Doctor Gold, and Doctor Yeats, who owned the practice. There was also a Mrs Yeats. When Clarisse and her mother bumped into Mrs Yeats in their street, she was always accompanied by four Pekinese dogs on leads, and in winter always wore a mink hat and coat. She made a fuss of Clarisse:

'Oh, how pretty you look with your lovely ringlets and bows, and what lovely clothes your mother buys for you.'

Clarisse enjoyed these compliments and her initial fear of doctors always subsided when she saw any of the three avuncular doctors. They were like part of her extended family but the doctors had all sadly, long since retired or passed away.

Dr Linley, her mother's present doctor, was a much younger woman and they were on friendly terms. Clarisse expected to see Dr Linley at the same time as her mother. But when her mother entered Dr Linley's office, the old receptionist silently ushered her into a different room. She felt alone and abandoned; this was the first time she had visited a doctor without her mother being present. She perceived a man with a wispy beard, in his thirties or forties, sitting behind a large, surprisingly empty desk in a sparsely furnished, neat and tidy room. He was thin with lank mousy hair and wore a shabby grey worsted suit. He looked disagreeable, almost sinister.

'Hello, I'm Dr Willis. Shut the door and come in.' He said not looking at her. 'Stand there,' he said pointing to the area in front of his desk. What can I do for you?'

Clarisse shuffled her feet, feeling awkward and tongue-tied.

'It's just a bad cold, or maybe it's 'flu'. Mum says I've got a high temperature.'

She felt such a fraud – she wasn't ill at all. The doctor got up and walked towards her, his eyes still not in direct contact with hers. He was looking down at her chest and he said in a casual tone:

'Take off your top and bra.'

Strange. Her chest didn't hurt and she didn't have a cough. Yet she did as she was told and pulled her school tie over her head, getting it stuck on her ear. She wrestled it free, then looking down, unbuttoned her shirt and unclipped her bra, piling her clothes neatly on the nearest chair.

He bent over her and started touching her breasts. He continued to do this for some time, stroking and probing them very slowly. She blushed instinctively and her body tensed, she swallowed hard. This didn't feel medical … It felt wrong, but she couldn't protest. She was too shy and paralysed with fear – and he was a doctor – a figure of respect in the community.

After a while he stopped and said in a very soft voice:

'You will have to be careful. Your breasts could be prone to breast cancer.'

Did she misunderstand? What a peculiar thing to say. Maybe he said something more but either she couldn't or didn't want to hear. A mass of confusing thoughts were milling around her head. She had to get out of there. And any words she might have said dried up in her throat, like stale bread. She dressed hurriedly and walked out as fast as she could; battling with her tie, angry and frustrated. She felt powerless. Doctors were like gods – they couldn't be contradicted. It would have been difficult to make a fuss. He would have just said he was doing his job as a doctor.

He didn't even write her a prescription. When she thought about this episode afterwards she couldn't work out why he had said she could be 'prone to breast cancer'. How could he tell, and even if it were true, why mention it? It was completely out of context: she had a cold, not cancer. Did he want to scare her? He had said it purely to justify his actions.

Yet maybe she had been wrong and the doctor was blameless: he had behaved completely professionally and it was just her vanity that had made her imagine his impropriety. Her inflated opinion of herself led her to believe that no male, even a doctor, could resist touching her young, untarnished body.

She hung around in the corridor, feeling vulnerable and foolish, waiting for her mother. When she saw her coming out of the other room, she rushed up to her and grabbed at her arms. She had to leave this place immediately; she wanted to be kissed and cuddled, to be comforted and reassured – her mummy's little girl – as usual. They started the walk home, Clarisse holding her mother's arm very tightly, her knuckles white and clenched. She told her what had happened. She expected her mother to be outraged. Delphine stopped walking, turned to her daughter and said calmly:

'Don't be silly, a doctor wouldn't do that!'

'He did, Mum, he did!'

'You sure you're telling the truth now?'

'Yes, I *am*. We should tell someone!'

'I don't want to make any trouble.'

'Why not?'

I don't want to upset Dr Linley. What will people think?'

Clarisse shook her head, 'Mum, what d'you mean, Dr Linley?'

'Dr Linley is married to Dr Willis. I can't complain about her husband. Besides, he was just doing his job.'

Clarisse shouted at her mother, stamping her foot:

'Mum, it wasn't right! Why won't you see?'

Delphine had always protected her daughter, cosseted her, defended her. She was from the Mediterranean and had a reputation for being hot-tempered, fiery. She said things like: *'if any man ever touched my daughter, I'd keel him.'*

Well someone had touched her daughter. Yes, it was a doctor and although it could be considered a medical examination Clarisse knew it wasn't right. He had just wanted to touch her breasts.

'It's best just to forget all about it,' Delphine said flatly.

She was always so strong and fiercely proud of her family but now she was acting like a coward. Clarisse couldn't understand her mother's reasoning – she was nearly as bad as that doctor. She felt betrayed, by her mother, by the doctor, by everyone.

'I hate everyone, even my Mum,' she muttered to herself.

Clarisse in Potignac

Let the neck be free.
Let the head
Go forward and up.
Let the spine lengthen
Like a tree.
Let the back widen
And the shoulders too.
Let the arms lengthen
From the shoulder
To the elbow,
From the elbow
To the wrist,
From the wrist
To the fingers.
Let the pelvis widen.
Let the legs lengthen
From the hip
To the knee,
From the knee
To the ankle,
From the ankle
To the toes.
Let the mind be free from foes.
Let the body be free from woes.
Let the mind be trouble free,
Empty of stress and worry.
Let me not think about money.
Let me not be angry
But happy today

And blow all cares away:
The bad, the mad and the sad,
Thoughts of lust and the dust of the past.
Let the mind be strong,
Forgive; forget; move on.
Let me act patiently
Be kind and nice
Especially to Harry.
Let the mind and body
Combine in perfect harmony
And peace and in gentle release.

Clarisse chanted her mantra every morning at the end of her exercise routine in the mini gym she had constructed in her large study on the top of floor of their French house in Potignac. She had a bike, a stepper, an 'abs-cruncher' and a set of weights. The mantra was based on the Alexander Technique but she had added other elements herself.

She was happy with life in the small French village, even surreptitiously enjoying all the gossip. She had met new friends such as Beatrice, Isabelle and Marion, an old school friend, had turned up in the village as well. She loved coincidences like this.

*

Clarisse was now hanging out of her study window struggling to put up the *Paix* flag she had purchased in the supermarket. Millions of them had been sold and they were flying from many homes up and down the country. However as far as she knew, hers was the only one flying in the village of Potignac.

'Harry,' she shouted, 'can you come and give me a hand with this flag, please?' Harry Roberts, her husband was busy watering his vegetable patch in the garden. He grunted something unintelligible but nevertheless he came to her aid and managed to secure the flag outside the window with a wooden pole.

He patted her behind and went back to his beloved vegetable garden. Clarisse ambled down the stairs and went outside to admire the flag floating in the wind. Not only was it a symbol of her utter disapproval of Bush and Blair's war in Iraq but it was also a statement about her feelings for what was going on in Potignac.

The Iraq war made her so angry. She wandered down the garden to watch Harry. She wanted to talk to him about it. She had to tell him what was on her mind.

'Harry – this US aggression is so unnecessary and obviously orchestrated.'

'Yes, I know, they could have toppled Saddam Hussein so easily in the last Gulf war, yet they hesitated then.'

'It's obviously in reply to September 11. Bush wants to show whose boss and sequestrate some oil fields at the same time.'

'And it's all so undemocratic. The US presidential elections were a fiasco with George's brother in Florida rigging the votes and now here we are on the brink of a war which nobody can possibly think is right.'

'All this talk of weapons of mass destruction, it's obviously just a ploy.'

But what made Clarisse angrier still was Blair's pro war stance.

'But why is Blair so keen on this war – what's in it for him? What is he, George Dubbya's lackey or something?'

'Yeah, it's very puzzling. Why can't Blair be more like his European allies, France and Germany, and stand up to the Americans?'

'Yes, Blair had the opportunity to be a world statesman, a leader in Europe, and he's blown it big time. It's all so depressing.'

Clarisse had such high hopes for a united Europe and Britain joining the Euro, now it all seemed an impossible dream.

'Europe should be strong and united, against those Republican hawk bastards thinking they can control the world.'

'Yes, those neo-cons have a vision of global hegemony. They want to control the Middle East, bulldozing their way into Afghanistan, Iraq and more than likely Iran as well. Democracy should be won through popular uprisings – NOT when the bloody Americans decide it.'

'They did their utmost to crush communism and now it's the turn of Middle East dictators. They never seem to learn their lesson. OK, a dictator is not compatible with democracy, but the people should overthrow their own dictators, it should not be decided by an outside power. When I think of what happened when they got rid of Tito, all hell broke out in Yugoslavia…. And we ended up with wars in Bosnia, Montenegro, etc.'

'Yeah, they never think beyond the first strike – like a bull in a china shop. They destroy countries and so-called totalitarian regimes but the aftermath is always a mess.'

'Absolutely. Was communism really that bad? Now the Russian and Albanian Mafia are in charge, there's more political and religious strife than ever before, and have these former Iron Curtain countries really gained from the capitalist West?

'And the same thing is going to happen in Iraq; the religious fanatics – corrupt politicians, the criminal elements and the terrorists will take over. Oh, it's such a mess.'

Harry turned round; he'd had enough of talking politics with his beloved wife.

'She does go on a bit,' he thought to himself.

He bent over to start up his new toy, a new, shiny post-box red baby tractor. It had cost a fortune but Harry thought it was worth it. It could plough and cut the grass, and there were numerous attachments he was looking forward to buying. He seemed to have mastered the driving of it already. Clarisse looked at him with pride. He was stocky but still very muscular, not bad for someone past sixty, she thought to herself. She was a few years younger and she too looked young for her age. Some people in the village joked that they were mere youngsters and only looked thirty or forty. She thought that living here in Potignac suited them both. The air was purer, the way of life healthier with most of their fruit and vegetables home-grown and organic.

Neither of them had ever lived in the country before but they both found it very relaxing compared to the frenetic pace of London. Harry had been a civil servant for several years with the Ministry of Education and had the opportunity of retiring early. They had met at University College London in their first year and had been inseparable ever since. Harry had studied history and Clarisse had a degree in English literature. They married soon after they left university when she found a job with a children's charity. They had a son, Adam, in the first year of their marriage. Clarisse thought she must have got pregnant on her wedding night, or even before. She was never that good at remembering to take the pill.

Clarisse's mother, Delphine, looked after Adam when Clarisse went back to work after six weeks. Adam was educated at the Oratory, where Tony Blair's sons went some time afterwards. Clarisse despised Blair but she had never understood the animosity sparked by sending his son to that particular school. Many London Catholics sent their children there; it wasn't a question of geography as good Catholic schools were few and far between. And although Clarisse had problems with Catholicism she had actually enjoyed her own

Catholic education. The nuns had made her feel she could do anything she wanted and that being a woman was not a disadvantage.

Harry had been so thrilled to have a son: someone to share his sporting activities. But Adam had always had a mind of his own and wasn't interested in the things boys normally pursued. His main loves were mathematics and technology. All he ever wanted was to play on his computers. After university, he had worked in IT in Australia, Hong Kong, the Philippines and Indonesia. They rarely saw him now and had lost whatever intimacy they had once shared.

When Adam moved abroad, Clarisse and Harry had come to a life-changing decision. Their respective parents were all dead, they no longer had any deep ties with London and they both loved Potignac. They had visited it together for the first time on their honeymoon and dreamed of buying a house there one day.

And their dream came true. The house they lived in was on the edge of the village and had been owned by Clarisse's family. The run-down old house was surrounded by about an acre of land including a large vegetable garden and orchard. It hadn't been inhabited for years and had come on the market via a cousin of Celeste, Clarisse's maternal grandmother. When he heard that Clarisse was interested he said she could buy it for a very low price as he was delighted it was going to remain in the family.

They had spent a small fortune renovating the house and the barn and it was now restored to its former splendour. Harry loved his new home, possibly more than Clarisse did. They both enjoyed the hilly landscape, the brightness of the light and intense greenery, very soothing yet vibrant at the same time. Clarisse had never really understood why Van Gogh found the Southern French light so disturbing. She was much more disturbed by the cold, icy winters she had experienced in England. Clarisse's favourite seasons were spring and autumn. Summers could be too hot and the grass dried up, singed and shrivelled into nothingness. The air was arid and dusty with the incessant deafening sound of crickets, but in spring everything was blooming, the birdsong seemed more cheerful and melodic, there were flowers everywhere with wild orchids, fritillary, and shrubs bursting into blossom. In autumn the theatrical landscape was magically lit up as if from a mysterious source. This was when Harry went mushroom-hunting, usually with a French friend, and sometimes she accompanied them. It had been exciting to find her first *ceps*, and the *chanterelles* were so numerous she became blasé about them. On one occasion Harry found a dozen *impériales*, known in English as *Caesar's Mushrooms*. He did check with a couple of neighbours that he hadn't mistaken it for a poisonous variety and was so delighted with his king of mushrooms he did a little dance. In the market *impériales* could fetch six Euros for just one hundred grams. There was not much farming in the area, which was mainly made up of woodlands and olive groves. They had a few groves themselves and the olives were duly netted and collected and sent to the local olive-oil cooperative. In return they received a delicious litre bottle of the first pressed oil every year.

Clarisse did sometimes miss the cultural, buzzing atmosphere of London but they had so many overseas visitors from England it more than made up for this intellectual gap. They had also got involved in village affairs, especially with the restoration of the old theatre. The *Théâtre Charles Dullin* was the main source of division in the village; a 'mini Iraq' as Clarisse called it. One group of villagers was spending lots of money (they even had a grant from the Belles Arts) on reconstructing the stage and auditorium but another faction were very against the theatre and thought it waste of money.

Against this backdrop the theatre was now almost ready and the first production planned was Ionesco's *Rhinocéros*, the play about conformity and the need to belong to a group. Clarisse was very attracted by the theatre of the absurd: the way it explored solitude and insignificance of human existence and she herself had suggested the play and was in charge of stage management. Harry was playing the part of Botard and rehearsals had already begun. It was a great way for Harry to perfect his French, but secretly , he had coveted the part of Berenger; he thought he would have been good at acting the outsider.

Clarisse said with a touch of mischief that the play 'tied in nicely with the Potignac "provincialism"; to be like one's neighbour or "keeping up with the Jones's" in petite-bourgeois society.'

*

Adam had got married in Potignac and the reception had been held at the theatre. As his girlfriend, Annabelle was a New Zealander they had decided that rather than getting married there or in London, a wedding in France would be perfect. Clarisse's thoughts turned back to the wedding. Ironically, she never thought she would have to organise her son's wedding. Adam had always declared he would never get married but after being a very truculent teenager, he had turned into quite a conventional thirty-year-old. He had invented some architectural software which was very successful and he was now employed by a well-known firm of architects in Auckland. Annabel, whom he had met in Hong Kong, had been a teacher, but she was now organising lunches for an Auckland firm of solicitors.

Clarisse missed her son yet was extremely pleased that he had settled down and was enjoying life in New Zealand. Harry and she were making plans to visit them soon.

When Clarisse had stopped being busy with the wedding she and Harry had started to do the occasional bed and breakfast in the summer months, by word of mouth, rather than through advertising. It was usually people who had originated from the village and had no house of their own there. This was ideal as it meant they could go away to New Zealand in the winter if they wished.

*

My periods stopped when I was 49 so my menopause started quite early. I don't have many symptoms and I couldn't bear the idea of going on HRT. More periods and it would be just like taking the contraceptive pill again. And there really hadn't been enough research into the long-term effects of HRT. It increased the chances of breast cancer the longer you took it. No I really didn't want to go down that route. I feel fine in spite of the odd hot flush at night, but that's all. If I was at all worried about any other symptoms, I consulted 'Menopause Matters' on the internet…

Clarisse took care to keep fit and eat correctly. She had cut out bread and lost about six kilos. She discovered that this was unusual during menopause; most women put on weight. Her French friends were always complimentary: they liked her skin, her hair, her clothes. She loved their praises. And, surprisingly, her sex drive had increased much to Harry's amusement. Lately she had begun to wonder what it would be like to go to bed with another man. She discussed this with her friends but most of them said that they had lost interest in sex. Yet although Clarisse was the exception to the rule, they couldn't imagine her with a lover.

'It would have happened already, if you really had wanted it, and besides,' said Beatrice, one of her closest French women friends, 'you don't even notice when men look at you.' But her younger, newly-rediscovered English friend,

Marion, had encouraged her. 'Go for it,' said Marion more than once.

Clarisse was quite a shy person underneath her confident exterior and although she did notice some men looking at her, she always felt quite embarrassed about it.

Clarisse's new hobby was researching her ancestors, mainly her great-grandmother, Daisy who was Italian.

Daisy (her real name was Raiza) was her paternal great-grandmother but the details of her life were very vague. Clarisse had started to write a novel about her. She usually wrote in the afternoons in her study, sitting at her computer, looking at the view of hills and olive groves, trying to reconstruct Daisy's story.

She hadn't shown it to many people yet. Harry had skimmed through it and being the loving husband he was, had said very encouraging things about it, but what she needed was some real criticism. She worried about the historical accuracy.

There's the part about electric lights in the home of Leonard Bertaux, Daisy's lover and eventual husband. Albert, our local historian, says that electricity most probably hadn't been put into any house, even a large and grand chateau such as Bertaux until around the thirties.

Portrait of a Painter

Nothing has changed.
No terrible beauty born.
My life is still the same
Or am I different:
Crazier, nastier
And full of shit?
Maybe, but that's not it.
Most desires
Are never fulfilled,
We have to accept
We cannot always
Have what we want.
It is our egotism
That makes us false.
What I merit could be something
Else entirely.
I am a combination
Of many things.
Love a fraction of what
I feel about life,
About humanity.
However the death of love
Has taught me to be
Tranquil, accepting, easy, calm.
Loving is enough.
I cannot change the world.

Clarisse was walking down the lane to see her young friend, Isabelle. She had recently had a nasty shock and

Clarisse wanted to console her. She was so lively and full of talent and ambitious. She usually got what she wanted and Clarisse admired that. She herself had really just fallen into her life: met Harry, had a son, had an interesting job but she had never really wanted to push herself …and she told herself she had never wanted anything more…

*

Isabelle Dove fell in love with the back of his head. He was conducting Carmina Burana by Carl Orff, an outdoor production in the magical setting of the beautifully-preserved medieval castle of Baux, not far from where she lived.

It was a crystal clear night and a very gentle breeze danced invitingly on her bare shoulders. She looked stunning, her skin glistened, her hazel eyes sparkled and her long straight silky golden-brown hair swayed slightly across her slender back. The majestic castle was silhouetted against the navy-blue sky, diamond-studded with stars, and its tall swallow-tailed castellated battlements were lit up by the masterly lighting director. The stage was built out from the castle wall, on scaffolding, like a beach house on stilts. On the central part of the castle wall there was a projection of a ballet dancer dressed in scarlet chiffon, ten times larger than her real size, pirouetting along the medieval bricked floor. Crimson and gold banners were draped across the other two sides of the wall, slowly, silently falling, swishing in the breeze. It was an opera she had never seen before, a wonderful evening – an experience she would never forget. The music was so powerful, the performers so resonant and vibrant, completely at one with the conductor who was totally in control. He was not particularly famous, more used to provincial tours than big city performances, but for Isabelle he was a God, not Pan, but a new God of music. She breathed in and out deeply, exposing her breasts even more. She barely noticed the dignitaries in the front row, just two rows away from where she and her cousin sat. The mayor and the celebrity politician had acknowledged her presence (she vaguely knew both of them). They had looked her up and down in her low-cut black evening dress as she passed them in the bar area outside the castle in the interval. They were both handsome French men. She smiled at them but had walked by quickly. All she wanted to do was get back to the second act and concentrate on the conductor's wonderful head and digest what was happening on stage.

Afterwards she realised how foolish she was; she had never fallen in love with the back of someone's head before.

He had long, wavy black hair and it flopped around as he energetically conducted the orchestra. His back and shoulders were broad, muscular, and capable. But his hands were long and slender. She didn't care about his face, in fact when he finally turned round at the end of the performance it wasn't a conventionally handsome face. It was craggy and pockmarked, brown eyes too close together, his nose rather long and thin, flabby lips. She was only slightly disappointed that he wasn't better looking: it was an interesting face, full of character. She would like to paint him.

At the end of the performance her cousin, Simone was brimming with enthusiasm: 'It was fantastic, perfect!'

'Hmm,' she agreed, 'and I loved the conductor.' She quickly searched the programme notes. He was Italian but of Hungarian origin on his father's side; his name was Sergio Strauss. Funny name, she smiled to herself. She would look him up on the internet.

The day after, she found his biography and even his e-mail address very quickly. He was based in Milan. There was no mention of any family, only that he still had a flat in the Buda part of Budapest.

She would write to him. She e-mailed him that day saying she would really like to paint him and attached her on-line catalogue. She wasn't really a portraitist but had done a series of paintings of some of the villagers who had interesting faces. The catalogue contained various examples of her work and an autobiography:

My work is completely abstract. People should look at my work without attempting to verbalise what they see. I have no particular philosophy about what I paint. I do not belong to a school, or a movement. My paintings are about the juxtaposition of colour and shapes. I like to think that they are powerful, energetic, yet silent statements. Abstract artists in Cornwall such as Patrick Heron and Terry Frost have influenced me. Some critics have likened my canvases to the whimsical musicality of Paul Klee's paintings but I do not agree. The images are purely visual but I hope their effect is similar to experiencing a musical concert, an opera, or a film.

Three years ago Isabelle had moved from Cornwall to Provence, to the village where her maternal grandmother was born. It was like starting from scratch. She started working on some figurative projects, including a series of portraits and some landscapes of Mont Victoire. However she continued her abstract work and was having an exhibition in Aix-en-Provence.

Isabelle e-mailed the conductor an invite to the private view of her show which was to be held later in the month. She was absolutely overwhelmed when she got a reply from him – in English – a couple of days later, even though she had painstakingly written to him in Italian which she had studied at university.

'Thank you for sending me your catalogue. Your work is very beautiful and I would love to buy a piece from you. However I am not sure about you painting my portrait. It is one thing that I have always refused.

'I see that your next exhibition will be in Aix. I have another couple of performances of Carmina Burana nearby so

I will definitely be in the area. I will try and come to see you and your wonderful paintings.'

She was so excited. She so hoped he would make the private view. Then she tried to forget about him. It was difficult but she had so much to do preparing her show. She was very busy framing the last of her paintings. They were big, some nine feet square, or 2.77 metres as she had to remember to tell the wood merchants. She was showing twelve paintings in all. The gallery wasn't big so she wanted to show them to the best possible advantage. Any more than twelve would have made the space look too crowded. She wasn't known in France and she wasn't ambitious. She never thought she'd ever exhibit at a prestigious gallery in Paris but she didn't really care. She just wanted to have a show. She didn't sell herself well, like other more successful artists. She was happy just for people to see her work and if she sold a painting that was an added bonus. She had been much more ambitious when she was young, but now, after the break-up of her marriage to her writer husband, John, she felt slightly vulnerable and maybe too lazy to change her ways. Financially she wasn't that badly off. Her late parents had left her their London house which was now rented out and her ex-husband was still living in their place in Tintagel. She managed to live quite well in France, especially as food was so much cheaper here, even after the introduction of the Euro when prices had now virtually doubled overnight compared to the old French franc.

The day of the private view arrived. Isabelle was having a crisis. Luckily she lived on her own; she would have killed anyone who had come near her. But Simone, her jolly, raven-haired, and curvaceous cousin, had been brilliant as usual and had checked that everything was arriving on time: the free wine from a local *vignoble*; the bread, *paté*, cheeses and ham, and most importantly the updated catalogues which showed Isabelle's recent work in Potignac where she lived. Isabelle and Simone had to rush to the printers in Brignoles that very afternoon to collect them. It had been touch and go – they had to wait for them to be bound – but they were finally ready. Isabelle breathed a sigh of relief. It would have been a disaster if they hadn't been finished on time, and lots of money wasted as well. They drove back as fast as they could to Aix. Everything looked fine. Isabelle was pleased with her decision to show only a few paintings. There were no ornaments, no flowers, and no distractions: just the huge artworks in white space. She had even declined an art critic. It was *de rigueur* at these local shows – for some well-known art historian or critic to give a speech detailing the artist's works.

'It's a load of bullshit,' Isabelle said to Simone in English. Isabelle had told the gallery-owner that she would make her own speech. And so, at six in the evening when the gallery was already quite crowded with friends, including Clarisse and Harry who lived in her village, and some cousins, even some from England, Isabelle spoke hesitatingly in French, describing her latest works, and how she had started painting them at her house in Potignac. She didn't have a studio as such but the house that had once belonged to her grandmother had a very large open space at the top of the stairs, once used for storing hams and grain. It had dormer windows in the roof and was an ideal space for a studio. She explained how the light and the vivid colours of the French countryside had influenced her work. She also made mention of buildings in places like Baux and Aix which had enchanted her and how their shapes had influenced the structure of her paintings.

Just as she took a breath before saying she was also accepting commissions for portraits, she saw Sergio Strauss walk through the door. She went bright red and completely lost her train of thought. She then giggled nervously and carried on with her talk, saying the main thing was for people to look at the paintings and enjoy them if they could. Everyone clapped heartily and enthusiastically. Isabelle became even more flustered, but decided to go straight over to Sergio Strauss.

'Hello, I'm Isabelle. I'm absolutely delighted you could make it!' She said in Italian, still feeling herself blushing. He was even taller than he seemed on stage.

'Please, let us speak in English; I do so want to practise.'

'Okay. Would you like a drink?' He was standing close to her, and looking at her intently, his eyes smiling, yet his mouth looked cruel, she thought. Not typically Italian, he was too tall and his hair was long and untidy. And he was dressed in an olive-green shirt and orange linen trousers – very un-chic! She loved that. Usually French and Italian men were so conventional when it came to clothes.

'Yes, some water.'

As she handed him a glass he started to walk towards the biggest painting on show – *Galassia*. 'This is so beautiful. I will buy it.'

It was like a dream. The man she was besotted with wanted to buy one of her paintings and it was the one that had been inspired by the night sky at Baux castle.

'Let's talk about that later. I just wanted to say how much I enjoyed the production at Baux.'

'I'd rather talk about your paintings...' he interrupted.

'Okay, I'll show them to you.'

Acquaintances she didn't know that well kept trying to interrupt her. She politely smiled at them and persevered. She was going to do this thing and show him around the entire space. Clarisse looked at her, smiling. Simone beamed, her hands clasped together as if she was going to start clapping.

'It was interesting you said some people likened your paintings to music – well, I agree.'

Isabelle was crest-fallen, 'Oh no, not that old cliché!'

Sergio must have seen the look of her face. 'I don't mean that they are literally like music. I mean they evoke the same emotions as a piece of music. Although your painting is abstract, it's almost as if you can feel it, the joy, the excitement, the sensual pleasure of the colours, the way they vibrate – the same way as you experience a piece of music.

Isabelle agreed. She could have spoken to him all night about her work. But suddenly he stroked her arm and said, 'I'm sorry but I must go now. I'm meeting the lead violinist for a drink at Baux tonight. She wants to discuss a minor change I have asked for.

Isabelle felt a stab of jealousy. A female lead violinist, oh no.

'Hey, listen; why not come to the performance tomorrow night at Baux? See how they compare. Take these two passes and bring a friend. Meet me afterwards at the bar, and we can discuss the price for your painting and when I can come to pick it up. It should just about fit in my, how d'you say in English, four by four? It will be ideal for my apartment in Milan. I would love to take it to Buda, but unfortunately the place is too small. So will you come tomorrow night?'

Isabelle agreed: 'Okay, I will. My cousin Simone would love to go again too.'

After he left, she was visibly trembling with excitement. She pulled herself together and quickly went round the gallery, chatting animatedly to all her friends and family. This was the best day of her life. And she sold another three paintings, one to Clarisse and Harry.

After the performance the next evening, Simone who had driven there separately decided tactfully to go home. Isabelle met Sergio at the open-air bar and he invited her to a very late supper. He suggested she leave her car in the car park and he would drive her there in his Mercedes.

French restaurants normally stopped serving quite early but he knew a place in the hills near Pertuis that always managed to serve up a superb meal, whatever time he arrived.

This was no exception: they shared a huge *fruits de mer hors d'oeuvres* and then some spinach flan made from *pâté feuilletée* served with salad and cold potatoes dressed in olive oil and chopped walnuts. Over dinner, they agreed on a price for her picture. He would pick it up when he had time. She wanted to ask him about painting a portrait of him, and thought this was a good time as any. She knew he had reservations and wanted to find out why.

'No, absolutely not. I really don't want my portrait painted. I never have and I never will, even though lots of painters have asked me.'

'Why ever not?'

'Well, I don't like to be reminded of myself. As I get older, I don't want my image to be stuck in time. I don't want to see my younger self when I'm older. Maybe it's because I don't want to think I'm too egotistical, too narcissistic, I don't know, too materialistic to be interested in my physical self. I'm more interested in my mind, my music, not my appearance.'

'But what about photos? Surely you have lots of photos of yourself? You must have been photographed endlessly.'

'Yes, but photos are more transitory, more fleeting. They don't feel as permanent as a painted portrait.

'But if everyone felt like you, no one would ever have had their portrait painted and how would we know what people looked like through the ages. Painted portraits are still very relevant.'

'Yes, but I'm not a Roman Emperor, I'm not important. I am a music conductor. People don't need to see me.'

'But people see you on stage, in photos. I don't understand your reasoning. And I am very determined. I see this as a challenge. I will make you sit for me.'

'Look,' he chuckled, 'let's talk about something else. And maybe it's like Dorian Gray, it will bring bad luck, or worse, I'll make a pact with the devil like Faust and go to hell.'

They both laughed.

'But don't you like looking at portraits of other people?'

'Yes, of course, I do. I love paintings; I just don't like them to be of me.'

Isabelle knew she should stop interrogating him, he was getting annoyed. But she was like a terrier with a bone; she would not give up. After they left the restaurant he drove her back to where her car was parked in the castle grounds and gave her a long kiss goodbye. That night she slept very badly.

After that, they kept in touch by e-mail or telephone. He had more concerts in small towns in Germany, Austria and Hungary. Then, a few weeks later, he came to her studio and picked up his painting. She threw her arms round him; they kissed passionately and then made love. She wanted to devour him, find out everything about him. His loves, his hates. She still didn't know that much about his private life. He had a teenage son, Gianni, with his German wife from whom he was separated and they both now lived in Munich. He often visited them there so that he could see his son.

They joked about Carmina Burana. She had downloaded a translation from the internet. She showed it to him when they were in bed that first afternoon. 'For example, listen to this:

'"*Floret silva nobilis*" etc.:
The noble woods are burgeoning
With flowers and leaves.
Where is the lover

I knew? Ah!

He has ridden off!

She was astride him at the time and started making whipping movements.

Oh! Who will love me? Ah!'

'I love you,' Sergio said.

She kissed him and laughed.

It was all the 'Ahs' that made her weep with laughter.

The next time they met they argued about philosophy. He was passionate about Heidegger. She taunted him about Heidegger's Nazi leanings.

'But what he says is so true: the necessity of achieving an authentic existence in the face of the downward drag of the anonymous crowd – intense, significant experiences were important – the elusiveness of human existence.

'I think life is a metaphor – like morning and night' continued Sergio; he grabbed a book from his bag with earmarked pages.

'Listen to this' and slowly but rather cleverly he translated into English:

We are born in the morning – our conscience still asleep. Slowly our eyes open to the world and we go about our lives. In the midday of life, friendships and loves flourish, erotic ecstasies sparkle like fireworks. Suddenly between moments of joy and serenity, tragic events, rudeness, delusions, betrayals, and cruelty intervene more frequently, sweeping away the last residuals of childhood. The mystery of living encounters the evil of existence.

'This is good, don't you agree?' Isabelle remained silent, not knowing what to say.

'Somehow we reconcile the two but clouds start to gather and anguish begins. Cries, laments, storms, and cloudbursts appear on the open sea – and there is no safety net. Light is obscured by darkness…'

'What is this? Who wrote it?'

'An Italian philosopher friend of mine, he can be very difficult actually. He's '*fou*', how d'you say? Mad as a hatter sometimes, (that' right, yes?). He can be very bad-tempered and easily offended. I have had a few disagreements with him myself but I am very fond of him all the same. He is quite a charmer, his wife is a saint, believe me, but he is what you call a tormented soul and he has occasional flashes of brilliance. Now shush, and listen:

'*With night, energy vanishes, time and anxieties disappear and love is like the residue of blue ashes that eternally blows in the wind. Time obliterates everything – the precious jewels of life pulverised like fine grains of sand in an immense desert where night and day intermingle, obscurely glowing – where nothing moves and sounds flow silently.*'

Isabelle didn't know whether to laugh or not, listening to her lover in his hesitating, very accented English.

Finally she said: 'Well, compliments on your translation but I can't decide whether this is a complete load of old bollocks or actually rather interesting.'

'It is not *bollocks*,' he laughed, 'it's poetry, that's what Heidegger said'.

'I would like to read it for myself – in the original Italian – and make up my own mind,' said Isabelle, determinedly.

'And of course, at our death, we are completely alone too.' He sighed and seemed to change mood suddenly.

Isabelle found the subject of death rather depressing. She was too young to think about dying.

Sergio could be irascible and moody and was so wrapped up in his world, his thoughts and his convictions. There was never any doubt in his head about what he wanted to do in life. '*So different to me,*' Isabelle thought, '*always prognosticating, vacillating.*'

But she was determined about some things and with a huge effort of will she persuaded him to sit for her for a portrait.

She made a formal appointment with him when he would next be available. She had promised it would take two hours, three maximum. She would take lots of photographs and do some quick ten-minute sketches, and then finally a detailed sketch of him in the chosen pose.

She was nervous when he arrived but once she started taking photos she relaxed and so did he. She thought he would be irritable but he was gazing up at her with smiling eyes, quite at ease in the moth-eaten armchair. She wanted him to feel as comfortable as possible. She didn't want to make a flattering portrait. She wanted to show his imperfections as well as what she thought was his striking magnanimity and the intense gaze of his eyes. She was finished in less than three hours, and afterwards they made love on her studio floor. She was surprised at his spontaneity. He hadn't minded rolling around getting dust and even a little speck of paint on his very expensive cashmere sweater. He said when he wore it afterwards it would remind him of her; she was a little speck of carmine paint. Then he said very quietly:

'You know you can never be an important part of my life but you are in my mind constantly.'

She remained silent; she was content with this.

She worked on the portrait for about six weeks and was finally satisfied with it. She thought it captured what so fascinated her about him – his charisma. He had already said he wasn't particularly interested in seeing it and didn't want to have it for himself. She had already decided she would keep it and hang it up in her house. One evening she invited him for dinner and told him she had finished the painting. Beforehand she had thought about how she would reveal it to him. She covered it with a black velvet curtain. She unveiled it with a dramatic flourish. He gave it a perfunctory glance. She had made his eyes look straight out of the portrait, so it seemed they followed the viewer around. He shuddered a little but didn't say anything at all. There was an embarrassing silence.

'Let's open this bottle of Veuve Clicquot,' he said, 'and congratulations on finishing that damned portrait, Isabelle. Now you will always have something of me in the house. Better that you have it here. I would never hang it up in my place. It would give me – how would you say – the shivers?'

'Or the creeps!' she suggested. She was getting drunk. They had already finished the bottle of champagne.

'Okay, now let's forget about it – it's time to eat, my love.'

She cooked him risotto with *ceps* and a huge salad containing everything he liked. She had got used to his fussy appetite – no cucumber, no apples, no black pepper, only pink, no liver of any kind. They ate slowly, feeding each other and toasting each other with a bottle of Bordeaux rouge.

'To you,' he said, 'my darling Isabelle,' and he leaned over and kissed her on the lips. She was so happy.

Just then his mobile phone started ringing and he answered it with irritation. 'Ya, ya,' he repeated.

Abruptly he stood up, 'I have to go. I have to go to Munich.'

'Why, what's happened?'

'It's Jana, my, … wife, she has broken her leg. She is all alone in the apartment. She needs me. Our son is on a school trip and she doesn't want him to come back early, just for her.'

'But you can't go now, it's late. Why not stay here the night and leave first thing tomorrow morning?' pleaded Isabelle.

'No, I must go; she sounded so lost and vulnerable. She will be angry if I don't get there as soon as I can.'

Isabelle swallowed hard; he was talking about his wife as if she still mattered to him. This had been the best evening so far with him. She knew she would always be an insignificant part of his life: he was so famous, so busy touring, so many other people depended on him. She knew that she couldn't see him often, but when they did spend time together it was precious and she seemed important to him. He made her feel special. Sometimes he did say things to break the spell, like when she had told him she was in love with him and how she had been from the very beginning. He had laughed and although he had seemed quite flattered and pleased, he had said: 'I'm not in love with you in the same way,' and had ruffled her hair. Things were never simple; she didn't really know him. He had never really talked about his wife before. But after that phone call he had changed. He seemed desperate to leave.

They kissed quickly and he was gone and she knew she would never see him again.

No one knew exactly what happened. He was just about to arrive at Strasbourg before crossing the border into Germany. Possibly the other driver fell asleep at the wheel and his lorry swerved and ploughed into Sergio's four-wheel-drive Mercedes speeding on the outside lane of the motorway. He was dead when the ambulance and police arrived. His skull cracked open, his body broken. The lorry driver had concussion but few injuries.

Simone came round with the local paper occasionally and when she had seen the headlines two days later she had driven straight to Potignac.

Isabelle read the article in silence, stunned. Then she felt her legs go wobbly. Simone made her some hot, sweet tea and told her to lie down. But she couldn't. The night before after he had left, she had hung the portrait of him up in the living room. Now she sat on the sofa staring at it.

She wasn't sure if the likeness was accurate. He was smiling his cruel smile and his eyes seem to penetrate her. What was he thinking when he died. She hoped he had thought of her for just a second. She would never know what he had really been thinking. He always seemed rather distracted, preoccupied, absent-minded. She sighed.

'Well, at least I have the painting,' she said later to Clarisse. 'Maybe I would never have possessed him completely. He was too much for one person, he was shared by too many people, but at least the painting is mine.'

Clarisse knew that Isabelle had fought really hard to paint his portrait. She had succeeded through sheer determination and the portrait was an amazing likeness even though he had only reluctantly sat for a couple of hours.

'The painting is forever, darling Isabelle, people never are forever.'

Clarisse and Alain

Reflections of a fevered brain
(Men or pause?)
Now is the time to pause.
Perverse emotional upheaval:
Tormented, tortured melancholy.
Product of a twisted mind.
Such anger and sense of alienation,
Anxiety and feelings of
Worthlessness.
Life's futility.
And much worse,
My utter stupidity.
Is it sheer boredom?
The big, black hole
Of an inward-looking soul.
Not enough to occupy
A fevered brain or eye.
No real stimulation
In the isolation
Of this rural life.
The petite-bourgeois
Provençal stance
Of petite France.
The pull of two cultures
Belonging to neither.
In England I feel exotic
And much more French.
Moving here, I feel so English
Out of water like a fish!

Clarisse had a secret, well a sort of secret. It was just a little fun; harmless enough, but she hadn't mentioned it to Harry yet, nor Beatrice or Isabelle, and especially not Marion. She was exchanging e-mails with a man from New Zealand. They weren't romantic exchanges but she did look forward to receiving e-mails from him, then felt guilty afterwards. She had met him at her son's wedding; he was a friend of Annabel's parents. His name was Alain Hatier, of French origin, and a history professor at Auckland University. She had mentioned to him at the wedding that she was researching her French ancestry and was particularly interested in her maternal great-grandmother, Daisy. She was attempting to write a novel about her.

Alain had seemed very enthusiastic about it and had said that if she needed any help she should contact him and then he had held her hand and told her how lovely she looked. That had been about a year ago. She hadn't contacted him straight away, mainly because she hadn't written very much, but now she had virtually finished the first draft and had sent him the first couple of chapters.

Alain wrote back a very encouraging reply saying, '*I loved it – it's beautiful and really evocative of the French countryside where you live. It brings it all back to me – the wedding, the scenery, the food and wine, your wonderful hospitality and most of all, you, my dear. With affection, Alain.*'

She replied: '*I'm so pleased you like my work but what I'm really worried about are any historical anachronisms. There was one thing I was going to ask you – do you know when electric lighting would have been installed in French country houses?*'

He replied:

'I think it would have been possible for some grand houses to have their own generators. Faraday invented the electric generator in 1821 and Edison developed the electric light bulb in 1879. Love and kisses, Alain.'

She wasn't sure what to respond and mentioned in her return email that *'love and kisses'* might not be very appropriate. He replied that he couldn't write just *'best wishes'* when he thought of her, it was too dry and English. She sent him her next excerpt, deciding that she would delete the part about Daisy playing with the electric lamp. Clarisse wasn't an experienced writer and she was experimenting – playing at being a novelist – so she found it difficult to rewrite or change anything. She did some research in the local newspaper archives and discovered that the first electric lamps had been installed in Nice in 1886. Perhaps Daisy's house could have had electricity after all.

Alain encouraged her:

'Just write what comes naturally. Don't try and make it too artificial. Only put in what you are certain about, but as far as electric lighting is concerned, I think it is perfectly feasible that a wealthy family would have had its own generator.

I wanted to tell you that I am going to be in Nice for a conference next month, and it would be great to meet up.' And he signed his message – *'lots of love and myriad kisses. A.'*

Clarisse was irked. She decided to confront him:

'I would love to meet up with you, but please don't let's talk about kisses. Frankly I find it rather boring and I am just not interested.'

He wrote back:

'I assure you that you are not the kind of woman that I would give proper kisses to. 'Love and kisses' is just an expression, isn't it? Frankly, I am only trying to help you with your writing. There's nothing sexual about it. A.'

This irked her even more. Was he teasing her?

'If there was nothing sexual about it, how had it come up in the first place?' She felt stupid spending so much time mooning over this ridiculous man. She liked the occasional flirtation but this man was getting under her skin. Admittedly, he was tall, blonde, blue-eyed, clean-shaven, slim: the epitome of good-looking.

My ego is wounded; I'm annoyed he doesn't think of me as a woman. Don't men and women's relationships always have a sexual element?

She wrote back:

'Your frankness is refreshing but if you are saying you don't find me attractive, why not? And what on earth are proper kisses? I think as a woman I can be both intellectual and sexually attractive. The two aren't mutually exclusive.'

How the hell had she gone down this path?

He replied:

'I would love to talk about this kind of thing with you face to face. The conference in Nice is about Renaissance France and I'm giving a paper on Venetian art and how politics influenced the subjects the artists painted. I am free on Tuesday and we should meet up – it would be intriguing.'

She did get the train to Nice once but the journey took nearly four hours. She was planning to go to the English book shop there so she could take the express coach instead.

There's no harm in meeting him while he's here in France.

And then there was Harry. What would she tell him? The truth she supposed. She loved Harry utterly; they were like one entity rather than two separate people. She had always thought that if anyone, some crazy gunman or schizophrenic, ever attempted to kill or maim her husband she would throw herself in front of him to save him. He always protected her but if it came to the crunch, she would give her life for him.

And now here she was waiting for e-mails from another man.

Maybe it's the menopause. I need to feel sexually attractive to someone before it gets too late and Alain saying he wasn't attracted to me has really got under my skin. I didn't get that impression when I met him. Whatever the case, I can't stop thinking about him and what he said. I'm behaving like an adolescent; the menopause is like adolescence in reverse. All those diminishing hormones rushing around my body creating havoc and making me neurotic. It's pathetic.

I don't want to make a fool of myself. Menopausal women do, I know. I am both attracted and repelled by my French, undiscovered passionate side. I am trying to explore it but at the same time, I want an easy life, no complications, no lies. I want to be honest!

I wish I could stop this madness. But how? Are there any mental exercises I could do to forget him? I remember that film, 'Eternal Sunshine of the Spotless Mind', where entire relationships with former partners could be erased from the mind.

The control of one's thoughts is actually a fascinating subject. I could learn to lie on a bed of nails – that would certainly concentrate my mind.

*

Then she thought about religion. Maybe if she prayed to God – but Clarisse and God had never had a very good relationship.

Even though I was brought up a Catholic and educated at convent schools, my parents were not practising Catholics. They didn't encourage me to believe. Even at the young age of seven I had doubts about it all. I remember sitting in church one Sunday during mass and looking round and thinking this is just make-believe, God isn't really here.

These doubts had persisted all her life and for several years she had never been to church, only for weddings, funerals and the like. Now she lived in Potignac she and Harry did sometimes go to church on Sundays, purely for social reasons as it was the only time they really met up with the other villagers. She had always rather enjoyed the ritual of the mass, the dressing up, the bells and smells and especially the music and hymns. She agreed with James Joyce in *A Portrait of the Artist as a Young Man*. It was the ritual and sensual aspect of Catholicism that was attractive.

The elaborate appeal to the senses: the visual appreciation of the spectacle – the robed priest and altar boys or girls performing at the mini-stage of the altar, the ornate paintings and statues; the flowers; the organ or piano music and the singing. The pleasure one felt in joining in the hymns; possibly even the light touch and wafer taste of the host in one's mouth… (Although I never take communion, it would even more hypocritical.) The burning candles, the general overpowering smell of the incense and mustiness of the church building. Even the marble statues, their white coldness or contrasting garishness – part fascinating, part abhorrent. I have grown up with these customs, they're part of my life.

Even though Clarisse tried to deny the power of religion, it was ever-present. Yet she couldn't believe in an omniscient, supreme, powerful God who ignored wars, famine and diseases, usually in the poor and underdeveloped countries of the world. And then someone like George W. Bush comes along, the Anti-Christ as far as she was concerned, and starts a completely unjustified war in Iraq. And he a so-called 'born-again Christian'!

And all that Catholic rubbish about one should not sin in thought, word or deed. This never added up for her either. If you had bad thoughts and that was a sin, how could it be as bad as committing the actual deed? If she had thoughts about being unfaithful, which up to this point in her life, she never had been, why not go the whole hog and be unfaithful? Clarisse was having sexual thoughts about another man, so according to Catholicism that was a sin. It was bewildering. Maybe prayer was the answer to these obsessive thoughts she was having about Alain.

Dear God, please let me stop having these stupid ideas about him. But a God cannot influence my thoughts or make me deny them.

Clarisse wanted to be a good person, she didn't want to have sexual thoughts about another man, *'but how do you stop yourself?'* She was a heterosexual woman who was attracted to handsome men.

But it was really annoying to be obsessed by one man's e-mails, not even a bloody physical presence. Thinking occupied a different time-scale. I can have a million thoughts while doing one simple mundane task. I can think of Alain while I'm cooking or cleaning or ironing. I can be conducting a conversation but I can still be thinking of other things. People most probably think of three or four quite different things in the space of one second.

You can't stop yourself from thinking. There's no commandment against it: Thou Shalt Not Think! How do you expel, reject, certain thoughts? Think of a tree, think of a river, think of a colour, and expel every other thought from your mind?

*

Transcendental Meditation wasn't the answer either. She had tried it once with Marion in Aix. The teacher just hadn't been right for them and they had got the giggles.

She was reading Gabriel Garcia Marquez's *One Hundred Years of Solitude*. Colonel Aureliano Buendìa was a huge brute of a man who had many lovers and had sired umpteen children. He boasted that he had no feelings, no heart. '…

He had learned to think coldly so that inescapable memories would not touch any feeling.'

This should be her nightly mantra: think coldly, have no feelings…

The next day she forgot about mantras and decided to look up Alain Hatier on the internet; something she had been meaning to do for a long time. She discovered that as well as history books and journal papers he had also had published a collection of poetry. She ordered it from the very small New Zealand publisher's website.

The book arrived surprisingly quickly. Most of the poems were about the New Zealand landscape: the mountains, volcanoes, earthquakes, the geysers and hot springs. How nature was wondrous, yet cruel and indifferent all at the same time. Others were about rural, provincial France, or about history: the French revolution, Napoleon, the Résistance.

However the final poem was a love poem, different to the others, less complex and rather cheesy:

Looking into your dark brown eyes I see forest shadows.
Touching your silky red hair I feel flower petal velvet.
Smelling your skin I breathe this Garden of Eden perfume.
Hearing your sweet voice I think of dawn chorus melody.
Tasting your lips I ingest all the beauty you possess.
How could I ever stop being faithful to you, my love?
How could I ever stop protecting you, my love?
You are my life, my wife
Until my death.
And I would gladly die for you.

Clarisse found it inferior to the imagery and complicated rhymes and syntax of the rest of the poems, too slushy and sentimental. The book was dedicated to Chantal, so she guessed this was his wife.

So Alain was happily married. I wonder why he never mentioned her when we met at the wedding or in his various e-mails. Now, should I meet up with him in Nice or not?

She wanted to meet him – there were so many questions she wanted to ask him, not just about her work but about this bloody poem. She sighed; she didn't know what to do. It really would be better to forget the whole thing. But she didn't:

'Hi, I'm sending you another chapter. And yes, let's meet up in Nice. We could have lunch. I can meet you at the Cathedral at 12.30 pm. I also wanted to tell you that I have read your book of poetry! I loved the ones about nature…

See you soon, xxx.'

She was still struggling with the historical parts of her novel. She wanted to discuss what an American author who had written a book set in the period before the Russian Revolution had advised her. Clarisse was curious about writing in English when the characters were speaking a different language and wanted some tips so had written to her. This considerate woman had surprisingly e-mailed straight back saying modern expressions should be avoided and to keep the language as simple as possible.

*

The morning of her trip to Nice, Clarisse woke up after a restless night. She was terribly agitated about meeting Alain but she did want the chance to talk about books, art, theatre, cinema. With her French friends she discussed recipes, gardening, planting, food, the weather, the usual feuds about land and property; and, of course, the village theatre, but never anything about art, books; her writing or cultural interests. It had been a real achievement to get them to put on *Rhinocéros* but the villagers were very unwilling to discuss the actual meaning of the play; more involved in making rhino heads, constructing the stairs for the set and memorising their lines rather than thinking about the meaning behind them. There had been a little 'discussion' about one disparaging line in the dialogue about people from Southern France but Harry had insisted that they keep to Ionesco's original text.

She got up early and had a long shower. She took extra care with her hair and covered herself in body lotion, slowly massaging it into her skin. She peered at the puckered skin around her inner elbows and in the creases of her neck. Old age was creeping up on her. She had clear, delicate skin but little wrinkles, the signs of decrepitude, were already appearing. Still, she could still pass for forty; one crazy person said she looked 38... She thought they were either senile or blind.

I've never really had a strong sense of myself. When I look in the mirror, I don't see a defined person, I look blurry, unformed, but then again, that's usually because I've taken my glasses off and as I'm short-sighted it's difficult to see. Plucking my eyebrows is difficult, putting on eye-liner is a pain and that's why I've never worn much make-up. I can't see what I'm doing. Putting this mascara on is making me blink and now it's all over my cheeks.

*

She couldn't decide what to wear: casual, nothing too special. Harry joked about her extra make-up:

Tarting yourself up for lover boy, are you?

She smiled sweetly at him, raising her eyebrows as much as to say, 'Yes, so?' and shrugged her shoulders at him. But was she? 'No, of course not,' she persuaded herself. She had told Harry about Alain being in Nice and that she was having lunch with him to discuss her novel. She drove to Aix in her Clio to catch the early express coach to Nice.

The coach was surprisingly faster than the train and took less than two and a half hours, but it didn't follow the same interesting route through the Provencal countryside and went along the coastal motorway instead. Clarisse was blasé about this stretch of the French Riviera. Everything had changed so much over the years. The Mediterranean resorts were over-commercialised and gaudy, peppered with prime-coloured signs and slogans; no longer elegant. She particularly thought San Tropez overrated. It couldn't be seen from the motorway but she had been there once and had got stuck in a very long line of traffic slowly edging its way inch by inch to the popular resort. It was far too glitzy and over-run with day tourists, the 'bling-on-sea' of the South of France.

She whiled away the time by rereading F Scott Fitzgerald's *Tender is the Night*. It was set in France, mainly near Cannes… she had now reached the part where Nicole's incestuous father and the cause of her mental problems is revealed:

'We were just like lovers – and then all at once we were lovers – and ten minutes after it happened I could have shot myself – except I guess I'm such a Goddamned degenerate I didn't have the nerve to do it.'

*

Clarisse stopped reading; she felt nervous, butterflies in her tummy-type nervousness. She wished she could disappear. Practising the Alexander technique, it had had happened to her once. She had vanished. On the back of a motorbike as she and Harry were riding around a coastal road in Crete. It was windy and for some strange reason she started reciting her mantra and she disappeared into the wind. She realised then that life was so fleeting. One never knew what would happen next.

I've had an easy life. I've never really experienced bad things. I'm not emotional, I never cry. I have never stirred or overwhelmed a man deeply, completely. I know Harry loves me but it's a compassionate rather than a passionate love.

*

They had reached the outskirts of Nice.

She was always surprised at how enormous it was. It stretched out for miles and miles and seemed to expand even further every time she went there. The traffic was terrible but the bus was only five minutes late. She decided to take a taxi to the *Basilique-Cathédrale Sainte-Marie et Sainte-Réparate de Nice*. The Nice taxi driver got her there speedily. It was just after noon so she wasn't very late. It wasn't a particularly inspiring or grand church, with its rather odd detached campanile. There were no crowds so it was easy to spot Alain in front of the Baroque cathedral doors.

She had recognised him immediately. He was dressed in a sky-blue shirt, blue jeans and brown boots, pushing stray bits of blonde hair out of his eyes – his sky-blue eyes.

Clarisse's heart gave a thump. *Now stop it,* she said to herself. She walked up the steps towards him. He held out his arms and gave her a big hug and kissed her on both cheeks.

'You look wonderful, Clarisse.' He squeezed her arms.

So do you, she thought, but didn't say it.

'It's lovely to see you again, after all this time,' she stammered, thinking, 'E-mail man made flesh.'

He laughed, 'Well, it's lovely to see you too!'

'How's the conference?'

'Well, it's still going on, but I've given my paper, so I can take a few hours out.'

'What was it on again?'

'The importance of politics in Renaissance art.'

'Yes, I have often thought about that and that the religious subjects of the paintings were secondary to the political prestige of the artists' benefactors…'

'I don't know Nice as well as Paris, which is where I was brought up, but Matisse, one of my favourite artists, lived near here so I do have a soft spot for it. I remember the exhibition of his in Washington in the 80s… So, where shall we go for lunch?' he asked, putting his arm around her shoulder.

*

As they were walking down the cathedral steps, arm in arm, Clarisse received a call from Beatrice. Harry had been rehearsing at the theatre and had collapsed. And Clarisse's world collapsed too. Her knees went wobbly and she uttered the words: 'Sorry, I must go, it's Harry… She feebly tried to punch numbers into her useless phone as she rushed to the taxi rank. Her nightmare had begun…

Uneasy Lessons

More than friends.
Two proud people
Too egotistical
For this lover game.
But a very sweet state
All the same.
Most of all I want
What you want.
I don't expect a lot
In return.
To feel comforted
And not to yearn.
To hold your hand,
To feel your smile
Caress my face.
To feel your touch
With emotional calm
And tranquillity.
I don't wish
To overwhelm.
Yet I want to feel free
And not to be curbed.
Like you, I believe in
Spontaneity.

Marion Moreau woke up with a start. Bloody birds, why did they have to start singing so early, and what was there to sing about in this hell hole? And there was a big hole in her life.

She wasn't having any fun any more.

She convinced herself she was grumpy because she hadn't had a good night's sleep. It had been too hot. She rolled over and looked at the clock, it was exactly seven o'clock. Guy or 'Ghee', as he was known in the village, had already left for his shift at the factory. She had to get up early in any case; Ricky was coming round to look at the roof. Many of the roof tiles needed replacing, maybe even some of the beams had to be fixed, and he was giving her an estimate for the work.

She did her daily exercises, took a shower and looked at herself critically in the mirror as she did every morning: not bad, still slim with toned muscles, blue eyes and short blonde streaked hair. Sometimes she wondered what the point was of keeping in shape – she was pushing 50, for goodness sake. It seemed so old; however it didn't influence the clothes she wore: she still dressed like a teenager. She put on a low cut t-shirt with straps, some tight very short hot pants, and some high-heeled, impractical sandals on her feet.

'Oh God,' she said out loud. *'What am I doing here in Potignac in the middle of nowhere? How did I end up here?'* She asked herself this constantly. She was bored, bored, bored. She didn't even fancy Guy any more. The whole marriage had been a mistake. Second time lucky was not true in her case. Her first marriage had ended after two years and she had been determined to make a go of this one. Well, it had lasted longer, nearly six years. But it was becoming a torment. Poor old Guy, he did everything he could to please her but that was the problem. She didn't respect him.

When they had first met on that Greek Island, Skiathos, she had thought he was the perfect Frenchman: dark, swarthy, not too tall, witty and romantic. So different to Bill, who had been the first man to propose to her while they were both at teaching college. He had made her laugh. He wasn't particularly good-looking or intelligent, but she had thought why not, what the hell? Let's go for it. They had married in her parents' local church, and she'd had the whole works: traditional wedding, white dress – not virginal in her case – flowers, three small bridesmaids, cars, cake, champagne. She had enjoyed the day immensely but hadn't really given a thought to why she was marrying Bill. Just go with the flow was her motto. When she thought back to those long-ago days, the memories were very misty. Bill was nice enough but he had no ambition, no drive. For all she knew he was still working in the same primary school, where was it, in Acton or Tooting Beck? She always got them muddled. They had found a tiny bedsit in Tooting and she had done supply teaching for four years. Then, after applying for several permanent teaching posts, she got herself a job in an oddly named place called Quark, near Leicester but there didn't seem to be any point in their both going up there. So she found herself some digs and promised Bill faithfully that she would come down to London every weekend, already unsure if she would keep to the plan. She had felt quite relieved to get away from the claustrophobic atmosphere of the bedsit. That and the smell of stale fried food left over in the sink and Bill's dirty socks strewn everywhere. She hated housework and they had decided to share all domestic duties but somehow they never got done. So she made the move to Quark not quite realising what she would do next. She threw herself into her job. It was quite a challenge because the school was very small and she found herself acting as temporary deputy head until a replacement arrived. Sometimes she was just too tired to make the journey back to London and her visits to Bill got less and less frequent. The relationship just wasn't strong enough and they started to drift apart. She teamed up with someone she met in the local pub and Bill seemed to be quite happy living on his own in Acton or Tooting. Even though they had been husband and wife they now never even exchanged Christmas cards and their divorce had happened by default after the required period of separation.

But Tooting had been better than Potignac. At least she had lived in London before making the mistake of getting stuck in the Midlands. She should have realised that she would have hated Quark when it had such a ridiculous name, more like a supermarket product than a town.

After eight years teaching special needs children at the primary school she had moved to a bigger school in Leicester but she felt increasingly lonely: for all its faults she had found her job in Quark quite rewarding and had met a few men whom she fancied and seen a few times. When she moved to Leicester things became frustratingly harder. She felt isolated and the job wasn't as interesting as she had hoped. Teaching was becoming so bloody bureaucratic.

The first sign that not all was right was when the majority of head teachers retired in the early nineties. The Tories changed the retirement age and teachers were no longer allowed to start their pensions at 50 and many senior teachers fled, leaving the profession bleeding like a haemorrhage. Most of the people left in charge were so inexperienced at managing schools that staff morale plummeted. Divide and rule seemed to be the philosophy: each for him/herself and fuck the consequences. Be nice to the head and you might become head of department. Marion couldn't bear all that crap. She started to loathe teaching but what else could she do?

Meanwhile, government interference was getting worse not better and there was more and more paper-work for teachers.

'I think I had a nervous breakdown,' she confided later to Clarisse. She was also having heavy periods induced by fibroids in her uterus. It all got too much for her and she jacked it in, not even bothering to work out her term's notice, blaming health reasons for leaving so suddenly. It was true to a certain extent as she had to undergo a partial hysterectomy and the hospital arranged it for one month's time, quite a feat when she knew how long hospital waiting lists were. So she decided to get as much holiday as she could by quitting school at the end of the Easter term. She was 36 when she had the operation. She had never really decided whether she wanted children or not, had always been ambivalent about the whole thing. Now the decision had been made for her, it was actually quite a relief. She loved children; well she had to, working with them every day as she did. Yet she had never had any great desire to procreate. She thought people had children for all sorts of wrong reasons, mainly selfish ones. She was relieved that she would never have to be responsible for having to feed, subsidise and educate a child, and being pregnant and breast-feeding had never appealed to her either.

The operation was a complete success and her ovaries had not been removed. As she recovered that summer and regained her strength, both in body and mind, the relief of no longer ever having to suffer a heavy period was immense and she felt exhilarated. She realised that her health was the most important thing. She would never have children now but nor would she become a lethargic, sickly mother, too tired or too ill to enjoy her children in any case.

She arranged to go to Skiathos in the late summer and had met Guy who was staying at the same hotel. He was of French/Italian origin but lived in London. He was about eight years older than Marion, also divorced with a teenage son who lived with his mother. He too suffered health problems with a stomach ulcer and 'issues with his nerves'. He had lived in Tooting but was now living in Battersea. It seemed that they had lots in common. It was ideal – they started seeing each other at weekends after they got back from their holiday. She was still in Leicester but was thinking of moving back to London. They took it in turns to visit each other. Soon Guy suggested she move in with him. She did and a few months later they got married in the local registry office. Guy's father had owned a snack bar under one of the arches at Saint Pancras station. It was lucrative and Guy felt obliged to take over the business when his father died but he regretted not going to college or getting an office job. When they had been married about a year, the arches were compulsorily purchased by Camden Council and although the price wasn't as much as he would have got on the open market, Guy now possessed a tidy sum to play with. His dream had always been to go back to France. He and Marion discussed it and she thought why not? She was fed up with London, doing supply teaching and, hey, life was too short. She fancied a challenge and she had no real ties in England. Well not many: her now widowed mother had lived with her married sister in Sutton. Marion and her mother had not been close. Her mother had always favoured her older sister, Wendy. When her mother was diagnosed with ovarian cancer Wendy decided that her mother should move in with her, her husband and two little girls. Wendy was a wonderful wife, mum and daughter. She took all domestic crises in her stride, in great contrast to Marion, who had never been a home-maker. She and her mum had always rowed and when Marion had divorced Bill, her mother thought that was the last straw. She was the first person ever to get divorced in the Bolton family. She had sent both girls to that French convent school hoping to make ladies out of them. Well, she had succeeded with her elder daughter but Marion hadn't turned out at all how she had expected…

Marion hadn't felt guilty about leaving her mum when she was ill. She was getting the best of care living at Wendy's and they could all come out and visit if they wanted. But her mother never got the chance and died quite quickly after the diagnosis.

Guy had inherited a house via his maternal French grandparents just outside a village called Potignac. The plan was to renovate it and he and Marion would live there full-time. His son, Robert, could come out and visit whenever he wanted. So the decision was made. Marion and Guy packed up the few things they had. Neither of them was greatly interested in possessions, so packing didn't take long in Guy's sparse and 'unlived-in' flat. They drove to the South of France in Guy's big Volvo. Guy had waxed lyrical about the village of Potignac where his mother had been born. It was in Provence and not that far from the coast. He said it was a pretty little place and the views of the hills were lovely. When Marion arrived at the house on the outskirts of Potignac she agreed that the countryside was very nice but the village was very peculiar, nothing at all like an English one. The few houses in the centre were all crowded together in typical medieval fashion with the church of St Michel on a hill overlooking everything. There was nothing much else except for a small bar and an even tinier *alimentation générale*. Yet in spite of the sleepy aspect of the place Marion was determined to make her life here. She had studied French up to A-level so speaking the language wouldn't be a problem for her.

They spent the first few months getting the house in order. It had to be rewired and re-plastered. The small kitchen and bathroom needed modernisation. There were three good-sized bedrooms but Guy wasn't very keen to put in central heating. There was a wood-burning stove in the large kitchen and he seemed to think this was big enough to heat the whole house. Marion disagreed. The house, which was like a large bungalow, needed extra heating in the winter. By this time she had realised Guy was quite mean; basically he didn't want to spend the money.

'Guy, it's best to have the central heating put in now, while the house is being renovated, rather than waiting. You can't expect me to live in a house like this with no heating.'

Guy reluctantly agreed and they had radiators put in the dining and sitting rooms and two of the bedrooms, with the boiler in a larder-type cupboard at the back of the small kitchen. Guy said they could just have the pipes put in the rest of the rooms and add the radiators at a later date.

Like the other villagers, Guy prided himself on using the central heating as little as possible and preferred to rely on the wood-burning stove in the kitchen. But the months of January and February were cold and even he finally succumbed and turned the heating on. Marion didn't know what had hit her; it was like living inside a fridge. Their bedroom and sitting room were relatively warm but the bathroom and corridors were freezing. Guy had wanted to keep the original windows and windowed doors so there were terrible draughts, even with the blinds closed. It was the cold that had really put Marion off Potignac. When they had arrived there she had enjoyed the village. There was lots going on in the summer months but after passing a winter there she had changed her mind. She would have much preferred being in London, going to the cinema, or looking at the shops.

Guy had said there was no need for her to work here in Potignac but she knew she would go insane if she didn't. After six months living in France, she realised that there was a demand for English language teachers. She had never taught English before, her specialism had been art, but as a qualified teacher, she thought she could manage. She did some research and found a course-book for beginners. There were many factories around the town of Aix. In fact Guy had found himself a job in the local tannery. He didn't want to use up all the money from the snack bar and as the plan was to stay in France indefinitely he realised he had to have some kind of steady income. He thought his income would be enough but he could see that Marion was restless and when she asked him if he could find out whether there would be any interest at the tannery in her running an English course, he promised to do so. But he was reluctant for her to come to the factory and didn't make many enquiries. In the end Marion went to the valve factory called Valerie, a state-of-the-art modern building on the road from Aix to Manosque. After speaking to the head of the Human Resources department she discovered that they had recently been discussing just such a thing. She had knocked up a CV for them, adding some false details about her English teaching experience. Then, hey presto, they offered her a short-term contract for a trial period of six months. She would have to visit the factory three times a week to teach the clerks, the engineers and the accounting staff. It was just what she wanted.

For many weeks Marion was busy setting up lesson plans and course work. The courses were due to start at the end of September, so the second summer she was in Potignac she was surprisingly busy. When she started work she discovered she really enjoyed it – she loved driving down to the factory and teaching the adults, who unlike the children she had taught back home in England, were all very eager to learn. Most of them had terrible accents but one or two had studied English before and were quite advanced. She had to split them into groups of 'ability'. There was one young man, an engineer who was streets ahead of anyone. She decided that he deserved one-to-one lessons. That was the beginning of the end. The young man, called André, was very pretty, dark, curly-haired with green eyes and very long eyelashes. He was 24 years old. She arranged for them to have an hour-long private lesson every Wednesday, late afternoon. On their first lesson she realised she was sexually attracted to him. She couldn't stop staring at those lovely long eyelashes. He noticed the way she looked at him and invited her for a coffee after the lesson finished at one of the swish bars in Aix-en-Provence. She could drive him there in her car as he usually got the bus.

She agreed light-heartedly and rang Guy to say she was working late at the factory arranging another private lesson, which *was* true, she smiled to herself.

They sat and drank and smoked in one of the bars in the main square in Aix for about an hour or so. His English was even better after a couple of beers when he was relaxed and away from the factory. They talked about everything: French politics, how she had ended up in Potignac, his home life. It turned out that he lived with his parents, and that they were away visiting relatives. He invited her back to the apartment. It was set back from a square near a now-defunct church. Marion had never been into anyone's apartment before. In Potignac everyone lived in houses. This apartment was quite new inside although the building itself was 19th century and had been renovated. It was a typical tidy, quite tastefully decorated affair with a modern but small kitchen, a dining and living room area, and a bathroom all on one side. Marion was fascinated by the many paintings on the walls, rows and rows of them. They were all original, not wonderful, mainly pictures of flowers and landscapes, but some quite expertly painted. She wandered around the flat, which wasn't particularly large, while André made coffee. There seemed to be only two bedrooms on the other side of the flat, one for his parents and one for him: he had no siblings. She wandered into his bedroom and looked at the usual posters on the wall, women in various states of undress, racing cars, mountain bikes, and photos of Olympique de Marseille footballers. The room looked as if it hadn't changed in fifteen years. André followed her into his bedroom with a tray of coffee. They both sat on his bed. She ignored the coffee and stroked his face.

One thing led to another and soon they had undressed each other. He was quite inexperienced but very sweet. However, she did feel shy – she, Marion, who never felt embarrassed about anything. She had been to bed with younger men before but she was pushing 50 now. When it was over, he fell asleep immediately. She kissed him lightly on the cheek, dressed and left the apartment. She hurried through the squares to her parked car, wondering if anyone could guess what she had been up to. She drove back to Potignac as fast as she could, feeling ever so slightly sordid.

Guy was waiting for her, in a foul mood. He hated it when he got home before her but since she had started teaching at Valerie it was happening more and more. He was an 'I want my dinner on the table when I get home' type of man. She made some excuse and cooked him one of his favourite pasta dishes – spaghetti with tomato sauce, followed by duck pâté and some salad. Simple, but he liked things like that.

When Marion got to the factory one Friday afternoon a few weeks later, Jeanne, the head of Human Resources, called her into her office. They spoke in French.

'Marion, can you come in, please?'

Marion nonchalantly sauntered into Jeanne's office.

'Marion, I'm sorry but we have decided not to renew your contract. You have been here four months now but we don't really think it's working out.'

'But Jeanne, I've been working really hard, making the lessons interesting. Everyone seems to be really enjoying it. In fact no one has dropped out yet, which is 'pretty bloody marvellous', as we say in English…'

'Marion, we feel that maybe you are just a little too enthusiastic, especially with the younger men, shall we say?'

Oh oh, that was it. Someone had rumbled her. She and André didn't have sex that often, only once in a while when it was certain his parents wouldn't be at the apartment, but someone must have seen them.

'Okay, but the contract doesn't end until March, there's another two months to go …'

'In the circumstances, we think it better if you leave now…'

So that was that, Marion was out of a job again and she was bored, bored, bored. She had never imagined she'd end up being a French housewife stuck in a boring French village.

Then she remembered Ricky. And at that moment there was a knock at the front door. It was him. She liked Ricky, he was an alternative type of guy, lean and muscular, long brown hair tied back in a ponytail. She showed him the wooden step-ladder which led out of the dormer window onto the roof. She watched him climbing up – nice bum – and followed him out. She pretended she didn't like being up there.

'Oh, I nearly fell, I don't like heights,' she said as she hesitated in climbing onto the roof. He put his arm around her shoulders to help her out. She liked that.

The original roof was very simple – a structure of wooden beams inter-laid with vertical slats and then covered in three layers of overlapping terracotta curved tiles – Roman style although some houses in the area had roofs made of '*Imperial*' French clay.

She could see many broken tiles and rotting wood poking through underneath. Ricky suggested using the existing tiles which could be laid on construction board over new rafters. And this would mean only one layer of tiles would be needed. He also suggested a layer of waterproofing, a '*membrane impermeable*'.

'How much would all this cost?' wondered Marion.

'About 50, 000 francs,' he said, 'that's around 5,000 Euro.' The locals still talked in terms of French francs. Marion tried to do a quick calculation and reckoned that they could just about afford it but Guy would take some convincing.

Ricky also suggested the alternative of solar panelling but Marion knew Guy would not be interested.

'Look, I'll let you know. But please stay and have some coffee with me.' She climbed back down the ladder first, he holding her hand to help her onto the first rung. She was playing the helpless, fluttering-eyelashes female. French men seemed to like that; along with buckets of flattery.

She led him into the kitchen but then stopped in the doorway, making him squeeze past. She would have preferred one big room – the kitchen and dining room knocked into one, but the house had been done up by Guy's parents and Guy was reluctant to change it.

While she prepared the espresso coffee she asked him in French:

'Ricky, are you happy here in Potignac?' Ricky lived with his wife and two children in rather a grand villa belonging to his grandfather that he had renovated entirely himself.

'Yes, why do you ask such a question?'

Well, there's nothing to do here, with just the church, one shop and one dismal bar.'

'Yes, but we can drive to many cafés and restaurants. It's not a problem.'

'But don't you ever get bored?'

'Not at all, there's no time to get bored, I am so busy with my work.'

She knew this was true, he was in such demand. Builders were few and far between in rural areas such as this.

'Don't you ever feel like just taking off somewhere? I don't know – to Marseilles, San Tropez, Monte Carlo, the Pyrenees…'

'Yes, I'd love to, but when do I have the time?'

'Make the time, Ricky.'

The coffee was bubbling away in the espresso machine. She poured it out into two very small white china cups and handed one to Ricky. As she did, she leaned provocatively over the table thrusting her cleavage at him.

Ricky had a confident air. He was a man-of-the world type, and was not faithful to his long-suffering wife Catherine. He knew when a woman was making a pass at him, unlike some Mediterranean men he knew who were all talk and no action. He leaned over and touched her breasts.

Marion leapt into his lap and starting kissing him all over his face. Ricky was still holding his coffee cup and the little that was left spilled over Marion's t-shirt. 'Oh fuck,' she said in English. But it was a good excuse for her to rip it off, which she did, and she thrust Ricky's hands onto her breasts.

Soon they were rolling around the floor, kissing and panting.

'Hey, that's enough now. We have to stop,' she said matter-of-factly.

Ricky couldn't believe his ears. He was raring to go, completely erect and wanting to penetrate. 'Hey, what do you mean?' He tried to pull her back to the floor.

'No, Ricky, no. Stop now. Look, come back tomorrow, after lunch. I'll be waiting for you. You can let me know when you can start work on the roof. Yes, I've decided. You're right – we do need a new roof – Guy won't take much convincing of that, I'm sure.'

By her calculations doing the whole roof would take at least two weeks. And Ricky would be well and truly hooked by then.

Ricky wondered what the woman was playing at. Bored English women could be dangerous – she was driving him insane but he had to play it cool. So he agreed he would let her know when he could start on the roof. Maybe just telephone her.

'I can't come tomorrow – I'll call you when I've checked my schedules. Also it depends on the weather. We usually have two or three jobs on the go at once. It could be in two weeks or maybe more.

'That's fine, Ricky, she said leaning over and brushing his cheek with her lips.

Ricky couldn't decide whether he had missed out on some good sex or whether he had had a lucky escape from the mad Englishwoman. Still she was very attractive and he loved the way she spoke her heavily English-accented French.

'Ciao,' he said and pinched her bottom.

After he left, Marion was still very much on fire. She couldn't decide if she had acted too hastily. God, she had practically raped him, but she didn't feel at all guilty. Guy was neglecting her more and more, she needed to have sex and if Ricky was willing, why not? He seemed like a pretty cool customer. Some men would have been very angry when she had stopped so suddenly like that.

She had never done anything like this before in Potignac. It was all too incestuous. She supposed people would talk if they saw Ricky entering the house all the time…

She started preparing the supper and waited for Guy to get home. She had to try and persuade him that they could afford the cost of replacing the entire roof rather than just repairing it. She made as much effort with the meal as she could. She was not much of a cook, but frying a faux fillet was quite easy and serving it up with oven chips was no big deal. She decided to make Guy his favourite *ceps* sauce. She took some dried mushrooms out of a jar and soaked them for ten minutes. In the meantime she chopped an onion and a few cloves of garlic. She fried this for a few minutes. When the mushrooms had soaked for long enough she added them and let them cook slowly. Then she added a carton of crème fraiche. Guy normally came in at 7.55 exactly. He always went for a beer after he finished his shift with his fellow workers and he expected his supper on the table at 8.00. Tonight this wouldn't be a problem. Sometimes she was late, sometimes she even forgot and they had to make do with bread, ham and cheese or salad. But she was now actually making an effort. She stirred the sauce that was gradually turning thick and creamy. She fried the steak and popped some frozen chips in the oven. It was a question of timing really. When she concentrated it was all quite easy. At 8 o' clock precisely Guy was sitting at the table and Marion was serving him the steak covered in the luxuriant mushroom sauce. She had also made a salad of lettuce, onion, pepper and grated carrot. Guy didn't say much but she could see that he was really enjoying his meal.

'Ricky came round today to inspect the roof. He said it would be best to replace the entire thing.'

'Oh, he was bound to say that, wasn't he?'

'No, he showed me. It really is an appalling mess up there. The beams are rotting and when they are replaced insulation can be put in as well, otherwise it will continue to be draughty.'

'How much will it cost then?'

'I don't know yet. He's going to give me an estimate.'

'Well, I don't know.'

'Look Guy, I've already told him I want it done. It's money well spent, if you ask me, it's an investment.'

'I'll never sell this house. It's going to my son.'

'But I don't want to carry on freezing my tits off every winter in this damn house.'

'Okay, okay. Let's get the estimate and then decide whether we can afford it or not. But the winters are never that cold here. It's you, Marion, and all those over-heated rooms in England you spent a lifetime in.'

Marion smiled. It wouldn't take much to persuade him now.

At the weekend Guy finally agreed that in the long term they did need a new roof and when Marion told him that it was going to cost around three thousand pounds (a slight underestimate) his eyes didn't pop out as she had thought they would.

'Well, that's not too bad, it would have cost that in England about ten years ago.'

Marion couldn't wait to tell Ricky that he could do the roof. She phoned him on his mobile and Ricky said he could start working on it straight away on Monday, while the weather was good.

'Oh, that quickly, Ricky? I thought you said it would be longer.'

'Well, the other guys are working up in Grasse so it will just be me most of the time, but they will come and help me with the scaffolding on Monday.'

Marion couldn't wait. She knew now that Ricky had arranged it so that he would be working on the roof himself.

The scaffolding took hardly any time at all to put up. It wasn't like the British variety which had to be carefully erected. It consisted of free-standing metal frameworks. There were about twelve of them, six at the front of the house, and six at the back. The wooden boards were just laid across each part of the horizontal poles. It was all so easy, thought Marion.

Ricky started to strip the roof tiles straight away. They were lovely old terracotta ones and they would be used again once the new beams and the linings had been installed. He made neat piles of them in the back garden.

'Because I'm putting a lining on the roof there will be quite a few of these tiles left over. I will only need one layer to cover the '*ondule*' – which is like wavy composition board and very hard-wearing. I'll buy them from you if you like, they are always sought after. In fact I can use them for the house we're doing in Grasse.

'Anything you say, Ricky.' That was good, it meant the bill would be even less than she thought.

'Ricky, aren't you going to stop for some lunch?' She knew that French builders didn't stop for umpteen tea-breaks like their English counterparts. They had a long break at midday when they normally went to a restaurant to have a proper three-course meal with wine and coffee.

'Yes, I'll be leaving soon.' It was gone midday.

'Ricky, don't do that, I've got lots of food in, let me make you a quick snack.'

'No, I want a steak.'

'I'll make you a steak, anything you want. Please come into the house.'

Ricky stared at her and she gave him a big grin.

'Okay.'

Luckily she had some more steak in the fridge. She made a quick salad, and fried the steak in olive oil and garlic. She sliced a baguette and some fresh brown bread she bought from a baker in Aix (she did both just in case he didn't like brown bread, which most Frenchmen didn't eat). Ricky sat now at the table looking slightly embarrassed but he soon tucked in to the meal and helped himself to the flask of red wine Marion had put out. Ricky ate both varieties of bread and lapped up the juices from the steak and salad.

'Hey, this is really good, and I like the brown bread. Where do you get it?

'At a new bakers in the market square in Aix.'

'Marion, I didn't think you'd be a good cook.'

'Well, cooking steak is pretty simple, Ricky,' she said pouring him some more red wine. Do you want some coffee?'

'No,' and he grabbed her. She threw her arms around him and kissed him long and slowly on the lips.

Next thing they were in her bedroom having sex. She had a fantastic orgasm and screamed. Ricky screamed too. Then they both laughed. She was having fun. It was never like this with Guy.

'Hey, I'd better get back to the roof,' Ricky said, jumping out of bed and getting dressed.

Marion smoothed the sheets but stayed in bed.

'Well, you know where I am now.'

He laughed and said: 'Yes, I know, but I want to finish the roof as well.'

She got out of bed, still naked, and hugged him once.

'Okay, lover boy.' She knew that when he was working, he liked to concentrate and not be distracted. Lunch followed by sex was fine by her.

'Get back to work then. And let's have lunch tomorrow.'

'Yeah, sure,' he said kissing her neck.

That evening when he left at 6.30 he didn't come in the house. He called out to her that he was leaving. Marion had been reading inside the house, it was too hot to sit outside. She came out and waved. They didn't kiss or anything. She knew that she had to be careful; the village was full of spiteful gossipers. But she was feeling wonderful. Two weeks of Ricky, what bliss, she thought, but then what would happen after that? She didn't want it to end. She had to think of something.

On Sunday morning Marion walked into Potignac to buy some tea from the small grocer's. She heard the church bells ringing, or rather screeching, like seagulls, she thought. People were just climbing up to the church for Sunday mass when she saw someone who looked very familiar – a blast from the past. She walked over to her.

'Hey, are you Clarisse Villeneuve?'

'Yes, why it's Marion Bolton from school, isn't it? What a surprise! You haven't changed a bit!'

'I moved here last year with my husband, Guy Moreau.'

'What a shame we didn't bump into each other sooner! Well, we must have coffee soon and catch up. I love coincidences like this.'

'Yes, we must.'

Marion was thinking Clarisse would be a good ally and give her an alibi when she wanted to be with Ricky.

Clarisse hadn't heard all the talk about Marion, 'l'Anglaise', the gossip hadn't reached her yet. She was overjoyed to meet her old school friend. Clarisse had been in the same class as Wendy, Marion's older sister, but when she reached the upper sixth and Marion was in the fifth year they had become friendly by chance. Clarisse had preferred Marion to her more conventional sister and had always got on well with her. She liked her straightforwardness and had admired her light-hearted, flirtatious nature. Marion had been very popular with the boys in the school opposite theirs. She was so different to Clarisse herself who remembered feeling so gauche and tongue-tied whenever she met any boy.

When Clarisse and Marion did meet for coffee in Potignac's only bar, Clarisse confessed to Marion:

'I've always tried to hide my shyness, be more like you, outward-going and confident. I realise now that I have constructed my personality. Slowly built it up into an aggressive toughness. I think I did this out of selfishness, egotism, trying to overcome my overwhelming sense of vulnerability without any regard for others…'

Marion wrinkled her nose, bored with the way the conversation was going: 'Oh, Clarisse, don't be so introspective, enjoy life while you can!'

The Glass Café

Can't 'God' be a woman like me?
Why do we need
Gods/Goddesses today?
They only inspire depression.
Can't they just go away?
Once upon a time
They could speak to us;
Make love to us;
Injure us; murder us.
Ancient Greeks and Romans
Relished those divine
Games of love and war.
Now, they are more remote;
Hidden in our hearts and minds
Rather than the world around.
He or she no longer meddles
In our muddled lives, and
Merely ignores us mortals.
Yet believers can still excuse
Bellicose ambitions
And hypocritical acts:
All in the name of 'God'.
And what happens when like me
You have no faith at all?
Force-fed early prayers or mass;
Angelus bell at midday call.
Communion after confession, with
A desperate search for sins.
Penance, grace, absolution.

The body and blood of Christ.
Was it cannibalism manifest?
In my middle years
I fear there is no God.
Yet I feel more guilt
Now than then.
An unfaithful bride of Christ,
Going to church; the pretender,
Singer of hymns, lighting candles,
Inhaling odious incense,
Savouring biblical verses:
'Through a glass darkly'
Of St Paul.
So, if I am a non-believer,
Why do I think we are here?
Here to ask questions
Such as: why are we here?

I've always had doubts about religion. Even at seven, I remember sitting outside the confessional, waiting to have my confession heard by a crusty old priest. It was like a telesales conversation you hear these days. A rehearsed insincere speech, always the same sins, no real repentance. Thinking that no god really existed, just another fairy tale like any other…

*

'I was with another man when my husband died. I still feel so guilty,' said Clarisse, before taking a sip from her green tea.

Gabriel looked solemn; silent at first, stirring sugar into his overly chocolate-sprinkled, frothy cappuccino with his long, bony fingers. They were sitting in front of the vast picture window in the empty Glass Café overlooking the Dove River estuary. Gabriel spoke in a deep, theatrical voice.

'Oh, my dear, what did you say?'

'I said I was just about to have lunch with another man when I got the call about my husband, Harry and my whole world came rushing to a halt. I wasn't even with him when he died.'

'He died suddenly?'

'Yes, he had a stroke. Absolutely no warning. Such a shock.'

'And he died instantaneously?'

No, he was rushed to the local hospital and then onto Nice and died soon afterwards – of complications – before I got there. It was terrible. I have tried so hard to cancel those few hours from my memory. I can't bear to think about them.'

'Oh, quite so, my dear. My late wife died of breast cancer. It wasn't a shock, she'd been ill for two years, but oh, the shock from such a sudden death must be dreadful.'

'It was the worst day of my life. If I'd been with him … I was actually in Nice, not far from the hospital, enjoying myself. Harry was completely wrapped up in rehearsals at our local theatre. If things had carried on as normal I might have met this man again. Well, to be frank, we could have ended up in bed, but then again maybe not… I don't think it was quite like that, but I will never, ever be certain.'

*

Father Gabriel Monroe walked daily from Sturwich harbour to the seaside resort of Dovington on his 'morning constitutional', often reciting poetry silently: 'A poem is like a prayer,' he thought. He always bought *The Times* at his local newsagent on the way back. He had got into the habit after Jeanne had died. She had mothered him, almost smothered him with affection and attention. She wouldn't let him lift a finger in the house and had spoiled him with her *cordon bleu* cookery. During her final days, he couldn't cope and had a breakdown, but a flock of parishioners had rallied round him.

*

'You were lunching with a man, nothing more; you shouldn't feel so guilty, my dear. Just as we forgive others, we must also forgive ourselves.

'Blake says, "The glory of Christianity is to conquer by forgiveness."'

'Well, yes…but….' Clarisse thought Gabriel was a genuinely holy man. *I can't imagine him performing any bodily function, let alone committing adultery …* She could picture his halo floating above his ascetic head.

'… I do feel guilty! You weren't born a Catholic, Father – I mean, Gabriel. I *was*. The nuns at school made me feel guilty for everything: petty, venial sins; the sins of the world; not going to confession; not saying my prayers; for NOT believing it all…'

'Oh, don't you believe?' Gabriel cupped his hollowed cheek, peering at Clarisse with an intense gaze. She felt slightly embarrassed:

'I'm agnostic, or Catholic agnostic, I suppose… but the nuns brainwashed me. They said I could sin in thought, word and deed. I know it was only a lunch date but I was definitely having bad thoughts about my lunch partner… On the other hand if just thinking something is a sin then you may as well go ahead…'

Bless me, Father, for I have sinned. It is 50 years since my last confession. That claustrophobic little room, the light on or off indicating whether the priest was inside; or that self-standing wooden box I knelt at; the priest opening the purple curtain to reveal himself behind the grate – like a ghoul. Confession signifies automatic forgiveness for Catholics, but my guilt cannot be assuaged. Converts covet our guilt; perhaps even wallow in it…

*

When Clarisse ran along the seawall, she savoured the tranquil East Anglian landscape, thankful that wide, open unspoilt places still existed in this over-populated isle. She loved the shimmering silver light on the wet mud; the metallic blue water pools and the dull khaki mounds of mud popping up here and there at low tide. She liked being surrounded by the increasingly invasive mute swans and Canada geese; the solitary pair of black swans; fat fluffy seagulls, some black-headed; mallards; widgeons; godwits; turnstones; curlews and oyster-catchers, among many other unidentifiable wading birds.

She ran at a steady pace, feeling the relentless pad of her trainers against the ground, sometimes on hard concrete, at other times on soft, grassy earth. On one side sheep and cows were at pasture and on the other – the salt marsh eased itself away from the wide river and pointillist buildings on the opposite bank. She felt a peaceful isolation: inhaling the bracing, yet alluring air; joyful to be alive, to observe, to think.

At home, in her flat alone, she felt the despair of Harry's loss: his clever talk and sense of humour; the way he enjoyed her cooking; his cuddles. Tearful at the unbearable memory of that abrupt French doctor announcing that Harry was already dead: lying out in his starched blue hospital gown, his hazel-brown eyes open and vacant; no longer there. Sobbing out loud, she tried to obliterate the scene and some days she even succeeded.

All the anger… the guilt… makes me spiral out of control. Simple, mundane things require so much effort and concentration. I'm grasping the metaphorical handles of my will, forcing myself to hold on to reality. Otherwise I would escape to another contemplative dimension. Life is a chore. Ashore the land of conformity I'm trying to forget the past… putting on my brave face…

*

One day, as a change, Clarisse ran along the promenade from Dovington to Sturwich port. Dovington had become rather run down since the recession but Sturwich hosted many pubs and restaurants, although even here some had closed down. The sun was high in the clear blue sky but the north wind was bitterly cold. Over her black tracksuit, she'd wrapped her beloved merino and possum scarf several times round her neck. Adam, her son, had recently posted it to her from New Zealand. It was lavender – like sea lavender. She was running around the surprisingly sharp bend just before Sturwich harbour. This was where the dummy fort or 'pill box', had been built for machine guns but never used and where the break water – called the 'Stone Pier' protruded onto the truculent waters. As Clarisse turned her head towards the salty seaweed sea – like a soup, the aroma of which she inhaled very deeply – she bumped into Father Gabriel.

'Ah, terribly sorry!'

'That's all right. Oh, it's Clarisse, isn't it?'

'Why, yes, you're Father Gabriel!'

'Call me *Gabriel*.'

Gabriel wore a heavy, grey tweed coat and brown corduroy trousers. Clarisse spotted his dog-collar peeping out from under his grey woollen scarf. He seemed pleased to see her, even though they had only met once at Harry's memorial service.

'Would you like to have coffee sometime?' Clarisse asked him. He was an intriguing man: an Anglican vicar, now a Roman Catholic priest. Someone who might listen – and she had some questions for him too.

'Oh, yes, that would be lovely. How about tomorrow?'

*

So the very next day they met early morning at The Salt Marsh Glass Café in Nettlebury. After much local protest, the café had been constructed, defiantly, on the beach. It was an elongated wooden-boarded construction on piles, with gigantic glass windows inserted along three of its walls. In spite of the unpopularity of its first, money-grabbing, regulations-blind owner, nicknamed 'the witch', it was now 'under new management' and thriving. Gabriel had suggested going there. As they entered, Clarisse looked around, surveying the distant rusty red, pale orange, sky-blue or navy blue containers lined up at the docks; the cranes looming over the steel-grey horizon and the ferry being piloted into the harbour. And in contrast, on the other side – the unthreatening salt marsh with its sea lavender, sea pinks and marram grass, stabilising the shifting sands against the high winds with their large underground network of roots.

*

They were the only people there and she had blathered about guilt. *I'm being self-indulgent, just because he's a priest,* she thought; relieved when Gabriel changed the subject.

'My wife, Jeanne was French. When we met before you said you lived in France; whereabouts did you live?'

'It's called Potignac, in Provence, where my mother originated. I still have the house there but can't face the idea of returning yet.'

'My daughter Claire lives in Provence, not far from there. My wife's father was Provençal. Claire has rented a small property very close to where his family lived.

'Oh, like me! My son, Adam, lives in Auckland.'

'I don't recall seeing him at the memorial service.'

'He came to Harry's cremation in Aix but couldn't make another trip to Europe. Such a long way to come a second time and what with his work and everything I told him not to come… So we both have children living abroad. *And* we're both widowed as well.'

Gabriel sighed. 'I was priest in charge at Dovington when Jeanne died. I had no wish to live in the big vicarage without her so I retired and bought a small flat in Sturwich. It's not really done to stay in the same parish – and that's when I decided once and for all to convert. The Anglican Church was so divided, I decided to retreat gracefully.' They both ordered more drinks, but this time Gabriel ordered a white coffee with no froth.

'Jeanne left me some money so I have some extra income. The few other priests who left gave up their church houses and forfeited their stipends. Some rely heavily on charitable donations and they do get into debt, especially those with young children.'

'I was lucky we bought the flat in Nettlebury before Harry died. I moved straight here from France after the cremation. That's when I arranged for Father Christopher to take Harry's memorial service.' Clarisse sipped once more at her green tea. She didn't see Father Christopher Campion Hall very often. He was Gabriel's friend and fellow priest, an absent-minded, doddery old English Catholic. Gabriel had helped with the service and Clarisse had chatted to him at the reception in the pub afterwards. She had noted his tall, emaciated frame and bushy white hair, like the prophet Isaiah, she thought.

*

'Enough about me. What I wanted to ask was how he and other Catholics have reacted to your conversion?' She was determined to get him to answer her questions.

'Oh, Christopher's been wonderful. He, Jeanne and I were friendly for years. However there is discontent amongst some Catholics: the nuns who want to become priests, or ex-priests who left to marry who're angry we've been given special treatment. They all think it's terribly unfair. Actually, being widowed when I was ordained a Catholic priest did help.'

'Your wife would've been pleased.' Clarisse returned Gabriel's direct gaze.

'Oh certainly, we talked about it. She knew I'd come over to the "true" religion one day. Female priests were anathema to her too. We planned to go to Our Lady of Lourdes but she became too ill. She was a great devotee of Our Lady.'

'And how did you two meet?'

'At Sadler's Wells when I was a curate. She was nursing at the French Hospital in Shaftsbury Avenue.'

'Ah, the Sisters of Mercy in their enormous white headdresses. We called them "Butterflies"!'

'I took her dancing a few times, very reluctantly, at the French Club alongside Notre Dame Church in Leicester Square and that was it.'

'Harry and I got married at Notre Dame!'

'We were married in St Mary's, Islington. Claire was brought up Anglican – for practical reasons – and Jeanne always regretted it. When we visited her family in France we attended Sunday mass at St Michel. Come to think of it, you might know it.'

'Of course! You can see its tall steeple from miles around.'

'Claire's boyfriend's a violinist. He sometimes performs there.'

'There was a young violinist at Harry's 60th party. He and an accordionist were playing folk music and two women were clapping in time to the music, like percussion accompaniment.'

'Good Lord, I remember Claire telling me about a wonderful party! Is yours a big, detached house, quite high up on the edge of Potignac? The garden glittered with candles and party lights, she said, and a magnificent barbecue?'

'Yes! So Claire was at our party?'

'Indeed… as a clapping percussionist!'

Harry died quite soon after that party. Arranging the funeral, battling French bureaucracy, all that paperwork seems so hazy now. I can barely remember flying back with Harry's ashes to England and the vague decision to have the memorial service at St Michael's Catholic Church. Harry was an atheist. He had said he didn't care about funeral arrangements. As St Michael's was just 200 metres from the flat it seemed as good a place as any. All our friends and family were happy to make the journey. Everyone said it was a wonderful service and a great reception at the pub – everything so well-organised.

When I look back to the day of Harry's death, it's so difficult to play back the details. The temptation of Alain, my negation of how things happened, my feelings all stirred up, my guilt, my anger.

*

'Strange, these little coincidences… and, to change the subject completely: why *did* you become a Catholic?' Clarisse asked abruptly, again trying to meet his direct gaze.

'Well, because of women priests, of course. I've always been a traditionalist, on the Catholic wing of the Church of England. The Archbishop of Canterbury did introduce a covenant to allow for differences of opinion but it's proved too difficult to implement. There wasn't enough provision for priests like me to avoid coming under the jurisdiction of a female bishop, yet the issue of homosexual bishops – which I don't find such a problem – is still unresolved,.

'But what's wrong with female priests? And if they become priests, surely they can become bishops too! The Queen is head of the Church of England, for goodness sake.

The monarchy is more progressive than the clergy! I don't understand why people get so hot under the collar about these things.'

'Men and women are naturally suited to different roles and functions. Yet even if we disregard the differences between the sexes, I firmly believe that the ordination of men is an unbroken tradition. It goes back not only to the Apostles but to Christ Himself.'

'You sound like someone from the 17th century – the Queen Christina of Dovington. Sorry! I've always been intrigued about why so many famous people, well, like writers, have converted and now there's this whole new wave of discontent…'

Gabriel chortled and said: 'Oh, did you know Queen Christina met René Descartes? He was a very committed Catholic even though he lived in a Protestant country… I meant that Christ chose only men to be priests so I strongly feel we should continue this tradition. We can't abandon the 2,000-year-old understanding of the nature of the priesthood. Thank the Lord for the Ordinariate of Our Lady of Walsingham!'

'What the hell is that?'

'It's part of the papal move to accommodate Anglicans in the Catholic Church. A small number of priests started leaving in the 1990s and the Ordinariate of Our Lady of Walsingham, which is based in London, was set up in 2009. As former Anglicans, we still retain our own distinctive identity, preserving aspects of Anglican liturgy, prayer and pastoral duties after papal approval.

'And you know that Our Lady of Walsingham in Norfolk is a pilgrimage centre for members of the Anglican Church's Catholic wing and for Roman Catholics. It contains shrines of the Virgin Mary maintained by both Churches. Anglican nuns based there who would like to become priests are angered by the Ordinariate.'

'And so they should be. In this day and age, especially with the Queen officially head of the Church of England, women should have equal rights.'

Clarisse had a longing to prod Gabriel and shake him by his bony arms.

'We're conditioned, especially in Catholic countries, not to accept women in traditional male roles. Yet in civilised society, we have female monarchs, presidents, prime ministers, why not female priests. Isn't your disapproval just prejudice?'

'It's a matter of conscience. Oh, believe me, Clarisse, I prayed constantly to accept this radical change in the Anglican community but I couldn't and it was becoming too contentious. Fortunately, my ex-parishioners were very understanding. Some fervently agreed with me…'

'But it's odd that people still want to become Catholic. I thought Scientology was all the rage these days. It's good to know Catholicism still attracts those in need of expiation… But you, Gabriel, are an exception. I can't imagine you deviating at all. But, anyway, welcome to the Catholic club!' She patted his hand.

The inner male sanctum has been vilified. The Catholic Church is an elite club; its keys belong exclusively to men. Women are subordinate: their role is to clean churches, arrange flowers or coffee mornings or fund-raising; cook and run the home; have children and be good mothers like the 'Virgin Mary' or become nuns – just how his God intended…

*

'And women in a priestly environment create tensions. I visited a Catholic seminary recently and was struck by the male companionship, the relaxed atmosphere; a real communion in God,' said Gabriel, his hands held as if in prayer.

'I don't understand why people believe in a God at all.'

'God is a consolation and the gospels are persuasive. The Christian moral system is more powerful than others – and Christ is still a very charismatic figure.'

'But I practise the Christian moral system without believing there has to be a God or a Son of God or a Holy Ghost.'

'God makes sense of our whole experience and the mysteries of the universe. Without believing I would have no purpose – it's the most intellectually satisfying explanation for being. When I look at the intricacy of the world, it's like peeling skins off an onion: there's always another layer revealing something equally intricate and awe-inspiring. There's no other explanation for the beauty – and love – in this world. God is its personification.'

'I sometimes feel like the layers of an onion. And moral dilemmas about my choice of actions: selfishness or altruism, fidelity or infidelity, are such a burden. Yet not all of us feel compelled to make ethical choices. And do we choose a God or does a God choose us? Why should Christianity be the one, true religion when there are so many others?'

'Oh, I suppose we will have to agree to disagree,' he smiled.

'But what about transubstantiation?' said Clarisse sternly, determined to ask him another question.

'We aren't forced to accept all Catholic doctrine but it does make more sense of the mystery of the Eucharist.'

'Yes, um, right. But any religion has a lot to answer for. Fundamentalists delude themselves that they are doing God's work when they kill others.
Religious mania – all that hypocrisy – it reiterates what I've

always felt: we are basically corrupt and weak, susceptible to bribery and delusion.'

'Oh dear, cynical Clarisse!' Gabriel widened his eyes, which were golden-brown. She hadn't noticed before.

'And the Pope's stance on contraception, abortion, gays, HIV and the cover up on paedophile priests is just ridiculous!' She continued.

'Actually though, Christopher and I agree that traditional Anglican beliefs are basically the same as Roman Catholic beliefs.'

'I agree. Why can't pluralism be acceptable? Why are Catholic or Protestant labels so divisive? I've never understood why people are prepared to die for these labels. We should all stand under the same ecumenical umbrella.'

'Have you ever been to my old church, St Peter's, in Dovington?'

'No, never.'

'I'll tell you a story … It was in 1532, on a frosty, moonlit night that four men set out from Dedham on the road ten miles to Dovington. St Peter's was then an important place of pilgrimage because of the fame of its Holy Rood.'

'Sorry, but what is a rood exactly?'

'It's a large wooden crucifix – Christ on the cross. St Peter's had a 14th century model, mounted on the rood loft – a formal and symbolic means of dividing the nave and the chancel. The loft housed the medieval organ and occasional gospel readings. The small stone stairs leading to it are still there. The Rood was considered miraculous as it protected the church and thus its door always remained open. These four men thought this was scandalous idolatry and pulled the Rood down. They burnt it about a quarter of a mile away on the village green. The fact that it was burned to ashes proved that it wasn't miraculous after all and merely an idol. Not long after, three of the men were hanged but the fourth escaped and fled abroad. Those who died were soon proclaimed Protestant martyrs.'

'They're more like vandals than martyrs.'

'Indeed. At the beginning of the Reformation, when 'Romish' idols began to be destroyed, the four men who lived near Bradleigh, a town known for its dissent and connection to Wycliffe and the Lollards, were considered heroes by Protestant reformers such as John Foxe.'

'Because they burnt a cross?'

'The funny thing is that before I retired we planned to construct a new Rood with the figure of the Welcoming Christ. And if it *is* hopefully restored, its former destruction would seem rather ludicrous.'

'Ha! The folly of martyrdom. And now, Dovington's former parish priest's a Catholic!'

They both laughed.

'Unfortunately for 16th century Protestants, the Rood was a symbol of "Romish idolatry" for its alleged power of preventing anyone shutting the church door. Yet for the local population and pilgrims it was a talisman or symbol of protection more than an idol for worship. In fact I've just realised that the pattern on your jumper is like a cross,' remarked Gabriel.

'Yes!'

Clarisse was wearing a black mohair sweater emblazoned with a white cross knitted into its front. 'The symbol of the cross is so simple yet so powerful...' mused Clarisse. 'I wonder what came first, the symbol or the crucifixion.... Seriously though, Gabriel, why was the Reformation so bitter – because Henry VIII wanted to remarry? It was all about sex, really, or politics, like everything else. All those executions...'

'Things are never simple,' Gabriel said with a hint of surprising bitterness.

'And Catholics now have to make do with the monstrous churches of nowadays rather than the beautiful medieval churches of before. I can't bear the grotesque statues of the Sacred Heart and those chalky Madonnas with painted red lips. They seem so incongruous in a modern building.'

'Like St Michael's? It is rather hideous, isn't it? That pine panelling and those stunted, abstract glass-stained windows. It's more like a clinic than a church.'

'A clinic for the soul?'

'Ha, indeed!'

*

What is a soul?' Clarisse often mused. Perhaps some essence of us survives. We should all live good lives regardless of an afterlife and not demand instant forgiveness for our sins. We have to overcome our despair and bad fortune without a God ... Gabriel is obviously a very intelligent man but what is it with him and his God? A prop, like a walking stick?

*

'Gabriel, you know Christopher's descended from John Payne, the 16th century English Catholic priest martyr. I've always been curious about old English Catholic families. All those priest holes and priests they used to hide. The fact they sacrificed so much to keep their antiquated faith…'

'Oh, a very dramatic, dangerous period… even families were divided. Charles I was a devout Catholic but his sister, Elizabeth, was staunchly Protestant.'

'And d'you think if you'd been a cradle-Catholic like Christopher, you too would've become a Catholic priest in early manhood?'

'Oh, I think I would. The religious tradition one is brought up in is certainly an influence.'

'But then you'd never have married and had your daughter.'

'Oh, there is that.' Gabriel looked perplexed, as if he had forgotten Claire – and Jeanne – in that moment.

'Are you allowed to remarry?' Clarisse smiled at him, almost coquettishly.

'Not according to Ordinariate rules. I'm now committed to celibacy and if I were a young, unmarried priest I'd have to relinquish the right to marry in future.'

'But the apostles, except John, were all married.'

'St Paul wasn't. In a letter to the Corinthians he said: "I should like you to be free of anxieties. An unmarried man is anxious about the things of the Lord, how he may please the Lord. But a married man is anxious about the things of the world, how he may please his wife, and he is divided." And Pope Paul II was very clear about this too.'

'So that's that then.'

Clarisse finished her tea and prepared to leave.

Gabriel's rather dry but a sweetie really, even though he's decided to become a Catholic priest. In spite of everything, I like talking to him, asking him questions. I feel connected. He's made a huge change in his life. So can I.

'Well, I must be off, Gabriel' It's been very interesting talking to you.'

'Oh, for me too.'

Just then, a large group of noisy people entered the café.

'We must meet up again.'

'I'd like that very much, Clarisse.'

Bed of Nettles

Faith's Lament.
Her disappointment
Is palpable.
Her jaw drops
In bafflement.
She will forsake you.
You don't deserve
That so desired
Powerful position.
Don't be rash:
You are confused,
crazy, dull-witted,
Psychologically disturbed.
Yet like a demon
Dancing on fire.
You change from
One minute to the next.
Face the truth.
Your problems are
In your head.
So much negativity
About your life, your
Wife, age, lack of vitality,
Your complex personality.
I was mad to fall in love
With you. Reconsider
Any foolish action.
Please, please, please.
Or else I will lose

my faith,
Your fellow conspirator.
A traitor,
Caught in a web of guilt and
Depressive disease.
No longer the sainted
Knight she thought you were.
She feels only emptiness.
Her love for you somewhat less.
Then I hear
Your voice
And my feelings
Change again.
The taste is bitter,
Bad like you.
The dragon
Is not slain.

I wish this fog would go away, thought Victor Leach, stroking his well-trimmed beard.

When Sister Sonia walked into his small office at Colwich Hospital on the outskirts of the town it was precisely 8 o'clock. The door was wide open – a good sign. Victor was standing in front of his desk and she handed him his operation schedule.

'Hello, gorgeous,' he said, grabbing at her and burying his head in her ample bosom. Sonia pulled away from him, gently raising her eyebrows and smiling to herself; pleased he was in a good mood.

When the fog in his head hadn't lifted, he could bellow out:

'Go away. Leave me in peace, leave me in peace,' and bar her entry.

Victor could be charming or irascible and prickly, depending on the amount of fog affecting his mood.

'Dr Jekyll *and* Mr Hyde', Sonia had fondly christened him, although as a consultant he was always called 'Mr' and constantly reminded Sonia of this when she teased him. Some of the other surgeons at the hospital envied his success and easy charm in spite of his contradictory nature and he had made some powerful enemies over his long career. He considered himself a non-conformist, a maverick intellectual who despised social hypocrisy and petty hospital politics.

'Leave me now, Sonia, sweetheart. I really must finish this report. Oh, and when Grace arrives, tell her to come straight in.'

He had deep-set brown eyes, a grey beard and thick, rather long but perfectly styled white hair. He was putting on weight but was rather proud of his 'love handles'. He sat down, pushing his hair back from his forehead, typing away furiously on his keyboard, preparing his application to become the consultant breast surgeon or 'Head of Breast Services' of the autonomous breast unit to be housed in the new wing being built at Colwich Hospital: 'An epitome of excellence' led by a team of surgeons, both breast and plastic, with oncologists, pathologists, radiologists, radiographers, and of course – nurses (such as Sister Sonia) working in the new state-of-the art building. The new breast unit would be equal to the one at Camford University Hospital. He had dreamed of this for so long now, still unconvinced he would be appointed to run the show. The Health Trust had been extremely slow in ratifying the building of the new wing, let alone appointing the head of the breast unit. At every meeting, the item always crept off the agenda with other more urgent business needing to be discussed. At long last the new wing was being built but the breast unit to be housed there still needed the final stamp of approval. The poisonous political atmosphere at Colwich was such that some doctors would be quite happy if the new space were to be dedicated to another medical department. The whole affair was proving very exasperating, giving Victor sleepless nights. He was desperate to get it through before there were even more cuts in funding, government reforms or rather interference, and privatisation of services. He often worked past midnight analysing every detail of how the unit could be run cost-effectively and efficiently without the opposition getting their way.

In the meantime Victor continued his work as a breast and general surgeon. The women patients all loved him; he had a wonderful bedside manner, making them feel special and pampered:

'Don't hesitate to ask for anything you need. My aim is to look after you and address your every concern. My staff will treat you – um,' he turned his head to one side and waved his hands in the air, 'like royalty! You have my word, and if you have any other questions, you can always reach me on my mobile number.' He was always very free and easy with his telephone numbers – to any woman – including his patients. He was very *'touchy, feely'*; some women didn't approve and he did get into trouble with one patient, but mostly he was adored. Some females were in love with him, or so it seemed to him, and most of the time he revelled in the flattery and attention.

My fog is getting worse. Sometimes I would just like to disappear…

Victor's odd behaviour began to be noticed. He knew his violent mood swings could be diagnosed as bipolar disorder but he dismissed this. He felt that everyone had their own complexes and their own way of resolving them and he became rather good at concealing his moodiness a lot of the time:

'In life one does have to be a good actor, whatever one's job!' he said to himself and others. When it got very bad he just wanted to be left alone. He put his depression down to his work problems.

'There just aren't enough hours in the day,' he said to Sonia that morning, wearily. 'And all these damn delays with the new unit are making me anxious.'

As usual, Sonia made soothing, sympathetic noises.

'I really think the decision is imminent. It'll happen soon, I'm sure of it.'

'Well, let's hope so!' They both held up their hands and crossed their fingers.

Victor thrived on spending long hours at his work. Yet he was feeling more wretched and disjointed.

Every day my fog is taking longer to disappear.

Regrettably, Victor rarely had time for a social life. The only thing he enjoyed was a game of tennis during his lunch break.

Faith, his wife, rarely saw him but they usually managed to have an evening meal together. They were both on their second marriages and had been partners for ten years. Faith mothered him and ensured Victor's life ran like clockwork.

Victor was not that fond of his own remarkably sprightly mother who was half-French – after a row over family property – and some niggling memories from childhood: *she kept my wavy hair very long and one morning I remember she put me into a girl's dress making me so confused… maybe that's when my fog started… it's really her fault…*

*

Victor had adored Faith's mother, 'my little duchess,' as he called her and was as devastated as Faith when she suddenly died of heart disease. He kept a photo of her on his desk at his private practice in Colwich. He spent most afternoons there, if he wasn't needed at the hospital or attending conferences or teaching courses on bio-ethics to medical students in Camford; or writing. Victor had written several academic and surgical texts and ethical books. His latest one was: *A Dying Certainty; Assisted Death or 'Euthanasia'.*

Faith took charge of Victor's debonair wardrobe. She dealt with all domestic issues so Victor never had to lift a finger in the kitchen. Faith taught English full-time at Colwich Comprehensive and although her job was demanding she was always home first. She felt his work was more important than hers and quite early on in their marriage she had decided she would aid and abet him all she could. Faith had been very beautiful once, with big green eyes and a halo of blonde, curly hair, but life with her difficult husband had taken its toll, making her look rather haggard. Since the onset of her menopause she had lost interest in sex. Victor was so busy with his work that he didn't seem to mind.

Thank goodness, she thought to herself.

Although he was an imposing, complex man, she was still madly in love with him and very proud of his achievements. She had thought he would eventually become a top consultant at a London teaching hospital or maybe work in Paris as he spoke perfect, unaccented French, or so it sounded to her.

Victor realised his 'fog' had hindered him from becoming 'top gun'. He was 'a big fish in a small pond'. When he was depressed and didn't want to socialise, Faith learnt to leave him alone, sympathetically saying:

'If you are happy, then so am I. If you aren't happy, then neither am I. If you want to stay home, then so will I.'

Victor had a reputation for being a 'ladies' man' although he admitted he didn't understand them; sub-consciously he possibly even envied them.

'Women are wonderful creatures, but they are too neurotic, demanding, even aggressive, and others are mysterious witches…' he said often.

'Men aren't emotional like women,' he pronounced to a male colleague, saying female surgeons were pretty agile these days at climbing the career ladder. 'We hide our feelings and keep control, whereas women use their tears or their sexuality to get what they want.' His colleague stroked his chin, not really agreeing with this but hesitating to say so.

Throughout both his marriages Victor had embarked on quite a few discreet, short-lived affairs and now he found himself attracted to much younger women, never ones as old as Faith. His compliments were platitudes:

'You look lovely tonight, darling,' or 'What a lovely dress!' but he didn't 'see' her as a real person any more; too absorbed in himself and his problems. Faith guessed he had been unfaithful but she relished the fact he was very attractive to other women.

'Darling, I love women chasing after you! It means you were a "good catch"! I love you so much I could forgive you anything, darling, even adultery!'

And of course, as a breast surgeon it was part of his job to examine women's breasts. She surmised rightly that there was no sexual pleasure in this for him. He was a professional and could distance himself from any sexual feelings they might have for him. He was perceived to be a 'typical gentleman of the old school' and his sexual dalliances were always with women outside his professional capacity – women who fully understood he only wanted a short affair – but recently he hadn't indulged in any new affairs.

Victor was a conceited man. He liked to prove himself sexually, but since Faith had lost interest in sex, getting an erection was proving more difficult. He wondered where the passion had gone in his marriage. When they first met they had spent whole days in bed, usually illicitly in a country hotel as they were both still technically married to other people. Now sex with Faith was more about affection than virility. She was his best friend and they shared athletic pursuits such as tennis, skiing and swimming and both went to the gym whenever they had time. She also helped with the local branch of the breast cancer charity he had helped to start.

Victor was an avid collector of lions in any form and there were drawings, paintings and sculptures of them in every nook and cranny of his private office in the centre of Colwich. He was also passionate in his study of philosophy and religions, even the Bible, yet he professed to be an atheist. He never read novels. Faith thought this a great pity as *'good literature can succinctly explore the human condition and simultaneously expand the mind,'* as she often reminded him. She tried to encourage him to read a good novel when they were on holiday but he insisted on reading academic books. His all-time favourite expression was: 'I just haven't got the time!' even when sitting on a deserted beach in some exotic location.

Back at the Colwich Hospital where he worked most mornings and some nights, Victor was still trying to secure more funding for the new breast centre. A few weeks previously, a Senior House Officer had been appointed in the general surgery department for a six-month stint, with a view to specialising in breast surgery, overseen by Victor. Grace Saunders was tall and slender with a wondrous mane of long, thick, crimped blonde hair. When Victor first saw her he thought she was the most beautiful creature that had ever walked the earth. He hoped that Grace would stay on after her training to work in the breast unit alongside him.

Grace, however, made it clear from the outset that she wanted a purely professional relationship with Victor, who in any case she thought was rather too old. She had a young daughter called Sally and rushed home after work to spend time with her. Not long after her daughter had been born the very hard-working Grace had gained a First in Medicine from Camford. An article about her had been published in the local newspaper. As well as being stunning to look at, she was highly organised and efficient. She was keen to specialise in breast surgery and soon she and Victor were working very closely together. She helped him with his conferences and discussion groups on breast cancer, his articles and grant applications. Victor found her increasingly sexually attractive but he respected her wishes. One day it got too much for him and he kissed her. He even tried to tweak her nipples, but she grimaced and took his hands away. Yet she admired him professionally and she nursed him through the many setbacks he suffered in relation to the new autonomous unit at Colwich. Faith sometimes chatted to Grace on the phone and she invited her round to dinner but Grace always declined. Victor talked of the three of them going to London to lobby central government for the new breast unit but it never happened.

*

Faith was giving herself a breast examination one June morning in her Nettlebury home when she felt a very hard lump – it felt like a pencil stump – on the side of her left breast. She tried to remain calm and quickly rang Victor at the hospital.

'I've found a small but very hard lump in my breast.'

Within an hour he had rushed home and driven her back to the hospital for an examination and biopsy. Because Victor was who he was, he was able to act very quickly and in three days, ignoring the waiting lists, he was operating on Faith himself to remove her malignant tumour. The stitching was so neat it was almost invisible. Victor had never been keen on doing everything by the book. He knew it wasn't ethical and he shouldn't have operated on his own wife but he didn't care. And in this very personal case, his colleagues happily allowed him to ignore the rules. They had rather he operated on Faith than get criticised by him for not doing a good job.

Victor snapped out of his depressive fog. He took time off work and accompanied Faith to the best breast cancer specialist in London. Luckily she didn't need chemotherapy but it was arranged for her to have daily radiotherapy and some hormonal treatment at Colwich Hospital within a few weeks. Life settled back to relative normalcy. Faith took a term off school, enjoying her enforced leisure time going to the gym every day and generally pampering herself. She appreciated the break from teaching her large classes. She was more and more frustrated by her inability to communicate with the increasing number of immigrant girls who spoke no English, usually wearing the *hijab* (some looked great, admittedly) but some were hidden behind even more cumbersome *burka*. It had made her increasingly illiberal. She was impatient for her and Victor's retirement, especially now. The cancer had sensitised her, given her an intense and heightened sense of reality. Faith had always been a very straight-forward, no-nonsense kind of woman: she called a spade a spade and was very direct. Now she was more contemplative, wondering why she hadn't had children. She had always used a coil, and then it just seemed too late, and looking after Victor, who like a child, was very demanding. She mentioned it to her friend Maggie. 'There was simply no room for a baby *and* Victor in my life and now it's too late.'

She and Victor had travelled extensively but now she felt happier staying at home, especially with all the terrorist bombings and threats. She realised how precious her life with Victor was. All she wanted was to be with him. He had been so good to her in this period and her friends told her how lucky she was having a breast surgeon as a husband.

She could hardly believe it herself sometimes that he had chosen to marry her; he could be exasperating but he was the most handsome, dynamic and charismatic man she had ever met. When they first saw each other it had been love at first sight. Their love-making had been frenetic and although sex was less of a priority these days it hadn't changed her feelings for him. She had been in the process of getting divorced when she first saw him at a party in Camford. He was still married so it had taken a while for them to get together officially, both of them experiencing animosity from their respective families and friends made through their first spouses. Every day they had spent together since was a bonus for her, especially now after her ugly brush with cancer.

But after the initial scare and the operation, Victor changed. When her tumour was first discovered he thought he would die of grief.

'I love you completely – '*heart and soul*,' he told her. He had constant thoughts about his soul. He had never believed in organised religion and was convinced humans were genetically programmed to believe in a God or belong to a religion and practise rituals. Some people possibly retained this atavistic instinct whilst others were now more psychologically evolved. Intellectually, he felt unable to practise Christianity but this did not stop him from being very interested in spirituality. The philosopher in him continually asked, 'What makes people tick? What is the meaning of life itself?'

Normally he took any mishaps with a stoical pinch of salt but recently pressures at work and now at home had made him even more introspective, making it hard for him to accept Faith's illness.

'It all seems so unfair. Why have we been punished like this?' he asked himself. For a while he and Faith were closer than ever – connected very deeply, as he said. Their love-making recommenced and grew so tender, so affectionate, but then, all of a sudden, it stopped.

This time it was him. He had always thought Faith so strong, both physically and mentally, but he was finding it very hard to accept that she wasn't in perfect health any more. He had always admired her pert, athletic body, her graceful way of playing tennis and the way she could effortlessly swim thirty laps of the pool. But now he was completely undone. He started to confide in Grace. 'What will happen if the cancer reappears in the other breast?'

As a doctor, he knew this was a distinct possibility. As a man, he forced himself to stop loving her. He thought that by not loving her he could stop the pain of her foreseeable death:

I imagine her cancerous body getting weaker and weaker and me being helpless to do anything about it and the fog gets denser and denser and I can't breathe…

After a brief and quickly-arranged summer holiday in Corsica, Faith started her daily radiotherapy and Victor threw himself deeper into his work: he taught new courses at Camford and was commissioned to write a book on breast cancer surgery. His previous book project about the human need for religion had been abandoned when Faith first got ill. He concentrated on meeting his new deadline. He dreaded going home and spent more evenings at his sports club, withdrawing more and more into himself. The only person he could talk to was Grace. She understood him. His depression became overwhelming. Grace urged him to see a doctor, but he retorted:

'I can't bear the idea of relating my troubles to a dry, punctilious psychiatrist, and a female one would be even worse!'

Faith often teased Victor about his views: 'Darling, your views on mental health problems, like your opinions on women, are still embedded in the 19th century!'

'Anyway I'm too busy, I have NO TIME!' he said, obsessively. Grace had quite early on realised that Victor had the classic symptoms of bipolar disorder. He relied more and more on her to write up documents for him. Sometimes he could hardly lift his head from his desk he felt so tired because of his sleepless nights. Grace mothered him, protected him, just like Faith.

Her patients in the breast unit called her 'the angel'. She often reassured them, sometimes patting their hands before they succumbed to the anaesthetic with Victor expertly cutting out lumps in their breasts or performing total mastectomies.

Grace was Victor's own very special angel. He wanted her to hold his hand too. One day when they were both in his office, he felt restless, twisting his fingers nervously.

'My personal life is so stagnant, 'he confessed.

That morning Victor had stared long and hard at Faith and realised his feelings for her had changed: 'I love you but I'm no longer in love with you. You're too old.'

Poor Faith looked shocked and her face crumpled.

'Don't be stupid, darling, don't say such silly things and go to work. You'll be late.'

Victor meant what he had said. Faith was such a contrast to Grace, 'my Princess' as he called her and who reminded him of the younger Faith when he had first met her. Grace was in her mid-thirties, very young-looking and healthy. She was happy to work very long hours, taking time off only when her daughter Sally was ill, as she herself was never sick.

Grace said flatly:

'Well, maybe your relationship is at its natural end. These things happen. People aren't necessarily meant to stay with each other all their lives.'

Grace spoke with authority: her own marriage had only lasted nine days.

Victor and Grace

Rainbow of emotion –
Blind to all
This confusion,
Sure of my love.
Often I am a
Puzzled presence,
Delicate sensitivity
Sometimes apparent,
Other times
Not at all.
Yet my love is
Instinctive, uncontrollable,
Invisible, inaudible.
I can taste it, feel it.
And yes, I can speak it.
I want more,
More than you are
Prepared to give.
What you want
I am never sure.
Why do I persist when
I know I shouldn't?
Somehow I know
You care.
Your voice, your words,
Your look, your kiss.

The breast unit finally received ratification with Victor appointed as head of 'Breast Services' but Grace was not to be part of it. On the same day that the news was being celebrated she received a letter from the Health Trust confirming that she was being moved to Camford Hospital as part of the regional surgical training rotation which hopefully would lead to a registrar post. The day of starting her new job had still to be ascertained as a new system was soon to be introduced and was now in the transitory stage. Grace had applied for the move but she hadn't told Victor this. He was furious and did not join in his team's champagne celebrations. He had never enjoyed alcohol in any case.

He had finally got what he wanted but Grace wouldn't be part of it. It seemed he was being made to choose between his ambitions for the breast unit and Grace. But Victor needed Grace, he relied on her. He wouldn't give her up without a fight. His paranoia increased. He imagined this was the work of his enemies at the Health Trust. They were deliberately provoking him by getting rid of Grace.

If there is a God, he's punishing me!

Victor and Grace were in his office when she told him the news:

'Grace, I can't tell you how sorry I am that you'll be leaving! I really thought that you would be able continue to work with me in the new set-up. I can't lose you now!'

Grace, normally so aloof, smiled broadly and hugged Victor:

'Oh, I'll be really sorry to leave too!' She realised that she would miss Victor.

Victor took her hands and kissed her on the forehead. Grace looked up at him and then they kissed each other in a long, slow, passionate embrace.

Victor felt a great warmth and peace, but Grace pulled back.

'No, this is madness! We can't do this, please, Victor, no.'

Victor sighed.

'My darling Grace!'

He looked at her in admiration, so much like her namesake who had died tragically in that car crash after her fairy tale of a life.

'My darling princess Grace!'

Victor fantasised about carrying Grace off on a horse and disappearing into the sunset, but he couldn't leave Faith after all she had endured.

He shook himself back to reality. He gently took her hands again but Grace pulled away:

'Victor, I have to go now, and thank you. You're a brilliant surgeon.'

Victor also had to leave; he was due in Camford for a meeting in an hour.

'Don't worry – we will sort this out – somehow.'

Victor vowed secretly that, if necessary, he would donate a monthly sum to Grace so she could work with him or maybe negotiate with the Trust to extend her contract further by taking a cut in his own salary.

If Faith had known, she would have been livid. He remembered how angry she'd been about that old family house in France his mother had donated to his older brother. Faith was quite cautious with money and often chided Victor for his extravagance. Even though he was living in cloud-cuckoo land about financing Grace's job, he knew his hands were tied. If Faith caught wind of this 'fantasy' she would realise that there was more to it than helping out a colleague in need. Victor always lavished generous presents on people he loved. He had started buying little presents for Grace, nothing much at first: some scented candles, books on philosophy, then some expensive perfume and an amber necklace which he had placed around her neck, adoringly.

One morning in the hospital office, Grace and Victor were finally alone after a busy few hours of surgery. Grace told him she had received confirmation that she would be staying a further two months at Colwich, which had caught her by surprise. She wondered if Victor had pulled some strings. She felt flattered but it also meant she had more time to sort out her new living arrangements at Camford and find affordable childcare for Sally. It was too long a commute from the country village between Colwich and Ipchester where she now lived with her mother.

'I don't know how I can thank you!' she burst out.

Victor had yelled down the phone at the Trust administrator, using his powers of persuasion and not a little blackmail, until he thought he had got his way. Unbeknownst to him, Grace's start date at Camford had been postponed because of new government regulations, not because of his influence. Nepotism had to be avoided in the new scheme of things and men like Victor were considered to be of the old school, always trying to get jobs for their friends. However Grace would not have agreed to the 'service' post that Victor had suggested for her at Colwich. She needed the experience at Camford. It was every young doctor's dream to work at a university hospital and training posts were few and far between. She was lucky she had been chosen.

Victor looked into her big, sapphire-blue eyes and kissed her on the lips. He was filled with inexplicable joy. He also felt the biggest erection he'd had for ages.

'Grace, I love you. I would die for you. I want to be with you. Please, please come with me to my private practice this afternoon, so we can be alone together.'

'No, I can't. Sorry, I just can't.' She kissed him back quickly and then pulled away.

'I care about you very much but you *are* married. I have a small daughter to look after and my mother is expecting me any minute. She has to go to a school meeting.'

*

Grace's mother was a primary school teacher and she shared the responsibility of looking after Sally with her daughter. She would miss them both tremendously when they moved to Camford – although Grace had intimated that Sally could continue to live with her mother if that was the only financial option.

*

'But, there's one thing I will say, Victor: you said that your life with Faith was over. Well, leave her and then we can be together.'

Victor's elation deserted him.

'How can I say this to Faith?'

He wanted to leave his wife. He was in love with this delicious young woman. Grace wore her protective shell very assiduously and never gave much away but she had opened up to Victor. He could still feel her sweet-tasting lips on his. He wanted to make her happy. She hadn't been very lucky so far. She had already told him about her short marriage. While she was still at university she had met a handsome boy on holiday in Corfu. When they returned to England they continued to see each other as often as they could, even though he lived on the south coast. On one careless, passionate night they made love and she became pregnant. A hasty marriage was arranged at the start of her final year and nine days after the wedding he left her. He told her he wasn't cut out to be married. She gave birth with her mother at her side holding her hand – but no husband. Her mother took leave from teaching so she could look after the baby while Grace finished her degree. From then on, Grace constructed a shell around herself. People like Sister Sonia thought she was 'the typical ice maiden, cold and unfeeling'. She was good at working with very sick patients because she was detached. This detachment made her devotion to her patients even greater. But in darker moments she wondered why her husband had left her.

'Maybe there is something wrong with me. I feel very insecure with men,' she confided in Victor. 'I never want to be hurt by a man, ever again.'

Occasionally she went to parties, always careful not to give too much attention to any of the many men constantly flocking around her. She got a reputation as a prick teaser but she didn't care. Sometimes she agreed to have sex with a chap, but always on her terms. She wasn't interested in a permanent relationship.

She still kept in contact with her former husband. She made sure he visited their daughter even when he wasn't feeling up to it and sometimes they all went on holiday together: they were going to Paris at the Easter break.

Grace's feelings about Victor had changed: he was very accomplished and had a great intellect – and he had been very kind to her. Grace wasn't known for her good sense of humour but she could joke with Victor. Sometimes they locked the door of his office, laughing and joking like two children. She had nicknamed him 'Victor Mature' in one of their lighter moments.

'And what about Clarisse?' she asked him once. You two seem very close. I'm not sure what you two get up to behind closed doors.' Clarisse had popped in to see Victor a couple of times at the hospital.

'I only do it to make you jealous!' he said, giving her tiny little kisses all over her face.

She was very grateful to him and loved him in a way, but he wasn't the love of her life. Grace had left all that behind her when her husband deserted her. Maybe he really would leave Faith for her, but she couldn't imagine it.

Too bad if he doesn't. He's going to be far too busy organising the new unit in any case, plus he really is too old for me...

Grace would soon be leaving Colwich. She had to be pragmatic. She had to get on with her life and settle into a new job.

The Victor problem will have to wait.

*

Victor was in hell. Faith seemed oblivious and wasn't too concerned. She knew to leave him alone in moments like this. He spent every evening at his club and ate dinner there. When he returned home Faith was already asleep.

Victor agonised about leaving Faith but he couldn't hurt her; she loved him, and he still loved her but wasn't in love with her any longer. He had always thought that men love differently to women. Women love wholeheartedly with a mother's unconditional love for a child, but men's love is less encompassing. Yet he and Faith were true partners. It wouldn't be easy, for either of them. He wasn't very good at looking after himself or at the practicalities of life and he was her life – nothing else mattered to her.

Finally, late one evening, he plucked up courage to discuss it. Victor told Faith he was thinking of living on his own for a while.

'I don't know what's wrong with me, but I feel as if my life is at a crossroads. I don't know what's going to happen next, with my job, with my life. I need some space to sort myself out.'

Faith tried to remain calm:

'We could buy an apartment and you could go there when you wanted.'

'This really would be the end if we did. I could sleep at my office for a while.'

But still Victor didn't move out. And every morning when he saw Grace he realised how hopeless it all was.

'It's over. Leave her. We can't be together until you do this,' insisted Grace.

'It just isn't that simple,' he replied. 'I loved Faith so much, I was always faithful to her, well, mentally…' he said.

'But you told me it was all over now.'

'I can't hurt her like this. She's having a difficult menopause and she's had breast cancer, for God's sake – I can't just leave her.'

When he thought there was a possibility she would die if the cancer spread he had been utterly devastated. Now he secretly wished she had died, and then he could be with Grace. *Oh my God, what a disgusting thought!*

Victor channelled all his energy into his work. The day arrived for the new breast unit to be opened. Grace was leaving the same day. She knew she was a damn good doctor and she was determined to get ahead at the teaching hospital. It was a challenge.

Victor towered over her as she packed up her things in her small cubicle. She said:

'Either leave your wife or it's over between us.'

Victor blinked at her.

'Over?'

They hadn't made love. But oh, how he had fantasised about it. He would die thinking about it. Ejaculation was like a little death, '*la petite mort*' as the French say. The excitement he imagined at entering Grace… he had dreamed about it so constantly it seemed real. However, he was rather worried that he might ejaculate prematurely…

Victor tried to reassure her:

'Listen, Grace, I want you, I love you, I want us to be together. I will try and find a way to tell Faith, I promise.'

'No Victor, I know you won't. You would have done it by now. By the way, I got an e-mail from that French friend of yours saying how disappointed she was in you. You promised you wouldn't ever talk about us. It's a secret.'

'I didn't tell her about you. I told her I wanted to leave Faith, nothing else.'

Victor made a mental note to end his friendship with Clarisse:

She's been talking to Grace. How dare she? The French bitch!

'She said there was lots of gossip about us. Well, maybe we should just finish it now before it all gets out of hand. I love you but I can't see any future with you. Stay with your wife and run your breast unit. That's all you ever wanted. I'm just icing on the cake. I really appreciate what you tried to do for me but even you couldn't get me a job in the new unit.'

'Grace, my darling, I don't want it to end like this!'

He grabbed hold of her violently, pushing himself against her, clutching her breasts, biting her neck. He had to have her…

Grace screamed, tiny bursts of tears filling her eyes. She pulled away from him with all her strength.

'Leave me alone, you bastard!'

She had been trying to let them both off the emotional hook but his physical attack had shocked her.

'Get away from me.' She stepped backwards.

'Please don't say that. Look, don't shut me out like this. You know I love you, I need you. Come here, I'll show you how much I love you.'

He reached out and tried to kiss her more gently but Grace became rigid in his arms.

She gave him a long, hard look.

It's all too difficult. I couldn't live with a man like him. He can be downright nasty, jumping down my throat for no reason. I was right all along: loving a man just isn't worth it. And now he's violent too. There really is no future for us. Faith is welcome to him. Men are cowards. They either leave you, like my husband, or they become like leeches and can't let go...

Grace missed the irony of her simile.

*

'I must go now, Victor.'

'Please, no, don't go.'

'I'll phone you, Victor, okay?' But Grace had no intention of phoning him, ever.

That evening Faith had persuaded Victor to eat at home for a change. She wasn't particularly enamoured of cooking but she made a big effort and served up his favourite French meal – a cassoulet of duck breasts, thick sausages and flageolet beans.

'We need to talk, Victor. There are rumours going around about you and Grace. Is it true?'

'What? What d'you mean?' he sounded shocked.

'Are you and Grace having an affair?'

'No.' He stammered.

'Well, there's a hell of a lot of gossip going on about you two, according to Maggie. She rang me and said you were acting strangely when she last saw you – and that you'd told Clarisse you wanted to change your life and fall in love with a younger woman? You mean Grace, don't you?'

'Yes.'

Victor was actually relieved by his confession. He had hinted to a few friends that his life was in flux but he had never mentioned Grace by name although he knew there were rumours circulating about them working so closely together at the hospital. It wasn't the standard behaviour of a senior doctor, soon to be head of 'Breast Services' and his junior. His enemies had gossiped about them from the outset. For a long time, nothing much had happened between them then it was like a bomb exploding, his feelings for her had become so intense.

'I love her but I'm very confused.'

'Damn you, how could you do this to me, after all I've gone through?' – Faith started to cry.

'I know, I know, I can't live with myself about it all.'

'Well, it's got to stop. She's leaving in any case. Let that be the end of it.

'Faith, look I'm very upset and tired. I don't know what to say to you. Let's stop talking now, please!'

'Oh, Victor, she's not the right person for you, can't you see that? She's really cold and calculating. And she lies, you know, she has lied to me on at least two occasions, and I could never understand why. But maybe now I do. How long has it been going on?'

'Not long, three months, maybe. Nothing much has happened but I just can't help my feelings for her.'

Victor was crying too.

Faith made a huge effort to stop her tears and pull herself together.

'Darling, you've been under considerable strain at work and with my illness and everything. You seem to be in some kind of reverie but she doesn't really love you. Quite honestly, that girl is incapable of love. We'll get through this, I promise you. Can't you see how much I love you? I am willing to forget all this because I LOVE YOU so much,' she was screaming at him now, hysterically.

He shouted back, just to keep her quiet.

'Okay, okay.'

'Let your new job be a fresh start for all of us. Forget what happened once and for all. You'll get over her, I'm sure. Time is the best medicine, after all.'

Victor couldn't stop thinking about Grace. Faith was right on one thing: he had to concentrate on his new job; there was so much to do introducing new work practices and systems, and most importantly of all, integrating the patients into the new unit. He had no time to worry about his personal life.

One day Victor did phone Grace but she slammed down the phone. Victor rang back but she just slammed the phone down again. He finally gave up in despair. He would never have her. All that remained were his fantasies about her; they were so vivid he convinced himself he had made love to her, and in his heart he thought maybe one day they would still get together. Grace had left an indelible impression: his own princess, but there was no fairy-tale ending.

*

My fog is still here but I am strong, I can function nevertheless…

Even during his despair he acted on 'auto-pilot'. And he still lusted after much younger women, even teenage girls. When he examined patients of 50 plus, he had an inexplicable longing to hurt them, by pinching or twisting their breasts. On the rare occasion when he examined a young girl's breasts, he had a strong desire to smother them in kisses…

Faith continued to cosset him, reassure him and ensure his life ran smoothly, but after that glimpse of how distraught he would have been at her death she knew it was because he couldn't survive without her. This was selfishness; it wasn't because he loved her but because he needed her.

Clarisse and Victor

So cruel even though I deserved it,
Behaving like a spoilt child.
Sadistic pleasure in
Using those harsh words.
Rapier thrusts through my soul,
Deeply wounding s-words.
Battered, bruised, angry yet
Deep thrust in despair,
Embarrassed, pathetic wretch.
Losing my temper without remorse.
An imperfect deity,
Your cruelty hidden well below
That charming exterior.
God of War and Thunder
No more playing the pipes of peace
Crossing swords with the less
Valiant imagined 'Goddess'
Despising my weakness.
Playing a dangerous game,
Arousing emotions
Better kept under wraps.
Never wear my heart
On my sleeve.
Such folly, crass immaturity
For one such as me.
How could I have compared you to
The beloved never out of my heart.
What more can I do or say?
I feel so terrible today.

*

I can't be bothered with men, joining a dating agency, trying to go on a date, making stupid conversation, making a fool of myself. However I do need someone. That 60th party I went to last week. I didn't really enjoy it. I felt uncomfortable and lonely. I couldn't zip up the back of my vintage cocktail dress and there weren't any neighbours in except for a friend's son who managed to bust the top of the zip but he did get it up – eventually! And then five seconds into the party someone spilt orange juice all over it. What a mess and now I can't get the stains out.

I should put an ad in the paper, not for a companion, but for an odd-jobs man: someone to do up zips, to do jobs around the flat, run errands for me if I'm sick, hold my hand when I'm dying...

Clarisse was introduced to Victor formally at a fund-raising dinner in Nettlebury, for the new Colwich breast unit, by Maggie, whom she had met at the gym.

'But we've already met! *Enchanté, Madame Rissie*! Did I tell you my mother is half-French?'

Another coincidence... well, well, well.

*

One early afternoon, Victor was having tea with Clarisse in Colwich's '*Ye Olde Tearooms*' to discuss a medical article she was translating into French. He told her she was '*très belle, charmante et intelligente*' but in reality he thought her 'quite spiky and demanding' and had noted her scrawny, brown-spotted, bony hands. She must have been beautiful once and was slim and quite youthful-looking but her hands were a give-away. He guessed she was attracted to him and she could be the 'persistent, neurotic' type.

'I want to escape this hum drum existence – change my life radically – fall in love again – but at the same time

I'm scared by the uncertainty. I'm not sure exactly what it is I want. Maybe I'm too lazy to start a new life. I'm just a confused human after all – but I do feel I need to make a choice.'

Clarisse was flattered he confided in her but he was being deliberately vague.

'What do you mean, change your life, fall in love, who with…?'

'Someone younger!' he grinned. 'What I mean is that we all have many facets – we all have multi-personalities. And we try to hide our true feelings from each other but sometimes, maybe just for a minute, we do connect to another person and we want to change…' And then he dropped his bombshell:

'I, um, feel I need to leave Faith …'

'What! You can't leave Faith.' Clarisse had met Faith at the Nettlebury fund-raising event and had liked her.

'She's a very loving, honest, loyal woman. You'll never find anyone else like her. Hang on to what you've got. And she *has* only just recovered from breast cancer!'

'I know, I know. And where would I go if I left her?'

Clarisse realised it was poor Faith who was the real victim in all this. When her breast cancer was discovered, Maggie said Victor had sworn undying love for her – not any more though, it seemed. Faith was his mother, lover, sister, housekeeper rolled into one. Men like Victor married mother figures and their infidelities were an attempt to escape the 'parental' relationship.

Perhaps men like Victor have sex outside marriage to overcome the Oedipal complex. He really is mixed-up, acting like a teenager… how could he think of leaving his wife just after her illness?

She swallowed hard:

'Look, I'm sorry, I must go, I have to meet someone about a book translation, but if you want to talk more, I would really just listen, honestly… I don't want to be too judgemental. Freud said people just needed to talk…'

But when Clarisse rang him after that, he always said he was too busy to talk.

*

Clarisse had first met Victor quite casually soon after she settled in Nettlebury, at a ten-kilometre marathon – running the circuit along the river estuary and park – in order to raise funds for the new Breast Unit. Clarisse went to the gym three times a week but she had never before trained for a marathon. She was one of the last to finish. It had taken her nearly an hour and a half and she was exhausted. She threw herself down on the floor of Nettlebury Church Hall with her arms and legs spread wide, closed her eyes and took deep breaths.

'Phew, I don't think I could do that again for another few years,' she said out loud to no one in particular. After a few seconds she heard a thud, and a rather big man with white hair was lying spread-eagled beside her. Victor was puffing and panting, very pale and pasty-looking. He turned to face her and said:

'Phew! I just haven't had time to do any training for this but I thought I should show willing and join *you* women. And I was the last to finish!'

Clarisse laughed. She imagined they looked rather comical lying side by side like twin Saint Andrews being crucified. Victor laughed back and the colour came back to his face.

He helped her up and they went to get some cold drinks at the table provided and started chatting. She thought him very approachable and jolly. He told her his name and she realised who he was. She teased him:

'Hmm, L-E-A-C-H, I presume, or is it L-E-E-C-H – the old name for a doctor? Maybe you *are* a leech, sucking people's blood … still… hasn't done you much good today…'

They were around the same age; he seemed 'fraternal' rather than avuncular like the doctors she remembered from childhood – but she never really got the 'hang' of him. He was full of confusing signals. Whenever she saw him after that first meeting he gave her long, penetrating looks so she thought he was attracted to her but when she confronted him, he denied it.

'Of course not, it's only very young girls I find attractive these days!' he said, laughing. Even if it was a joke, it still made her angry:

'If a woman said that about young boys, there would be uproar!'

Yet – Clarisse had to be honest – she was attracted to Victor. She admired his height and broad shoulders even though he wasn't what she considered conventionally handsome. He had rather saturnine features, and she had never really liked bearded men: they made her skin sore. To top it all, he was rather large around the middle. But he wore it well and his exquisite clothes really suited him: Swiss cotton striped or denim shirts and beige chinos; soft leather tan Chelsea boots or brown brogues and either midnight-blue velvet or chocolate-brown corduroy jackets.

It seemed effortless, but he must have put quite a lot of thought into it. Strange, as he always said he never had time for such things. Dear Harry was never that interested in clothes. I enjoyed sex enormously but now it's not really important. I was curious about having sex with a man again but maybe I'm no longer interested… And Victor is as slippery as an eel, always changing mood or never in one place long enough. He's a proper 'prick'.

Yet despite the stupidities he sometimes uttered – there was a frisson between them. Once when she was wearing her driving glasses, he said she looked sexy. At other times, he said, 'Never rule sex out,' wagging a metaphorical finger at her.

'Look, I like talking to you – but we're just friends, okay?' she said, trying to convince herself, rather than him.

Clarisse had helped Victor with a paper about breast cancer which was going to be presented and published in both English and French as part of an EC initiative. They had argued about his insistence on calling the breast surgeon 'he' and a 'gentleman'.

'How can you possibly say that in this day and age? Even in French, one should say "*elle ou lui*", and "*une personne gentile*", not denoting gender at all. You really are Mr Victorian, aren't you?'

She wished she wasn't attracted to him. He was as arrogant as a 'peacock' who basked in the adulation of women. And she certainly didn't get the impression he believed in sexual equality.

They rowed about politics. Victor professed to be left-wing but she couldn't quite see it. He admired Rupert Murdoch and the empire he had created.

'Such influence in so many continents. The man's a genius!'

'Yes, an evil, devious, biased genius, with politicians and policemen in his pocket! My husband refused to subscribe to Sky television in France because of Murdoch and I never read The Times, let alone his other newspapers.'

She started telling Victor about Harry's death when she suddenly realised she hadn't registered with a GP:

'*And* I'm long overdue a mammogram.'

'Don't worry about that, I can organise one for you at Colwich.'

He telephoned her the next day with a date but when Clarisse turned up at the radiology department at the time stated, there was no record of the appointment and in fact the radiologist was on holiday that day.

Clarisse shrugged her shoulders thinking Victor an absent-minded 'professor' to have got the date wrong. She would register with her local GP. Hopefully it wouldn't be too long before she got back into the NHS system.

Victor rang her the following day, apologising profusely for the mix-up.

'I tell you what, come to my private practice in Colwich and I can refer you from there. Let's skip all this damn bureaucracy!'

They made a date for the following week and as Clarisse drove there, she felt apprehensive even queasy about this meeting. It was odd not to go through the proper channels.

She found the building very easily: Tudor in structure with its original chimneys, beams and lattice windows, but now converted into offices. Victor's office was in an annexe across a courtyard. She entered a small, overheated, cramped waiting room. It was filled with all sorts of lions including a stylised, medieval wooden carving used as a doorstop. Framed drawings and letters from grateful former breast cancer patients hung on the walls. There were two enormous black-and-white photographs, one of a naked one-breasted woman, the other of a one-armed woman playing golf. The claustrophobic, womb-like atmosphere and the heat were oppressive. Monotonous new-age music droned on in the background. 'What appalling taste in music,' she thought.

Victor came out of his office straight away, '*Riss-see, ma chère, bonjour!*' He hugged her and kissed her on both cheeks very affectionately. He always insisted on speaking to her in French – badly. She changed to English.

'Hi, Victor, what a lovely building!' She laughed nervously, still feeling uneasy about this unorthodox visit. She followed him into his office, also very cramped with just a desk and small examining table and shelves stuffed with thousands of text books – and yet more lions crammed everywhere. He showed her his book about 'assisted death' and insisted on giving her a copy.

'Dear Rissie, let me inscribe it for you.'

She watched as he wrote:

'To my darling Rissie, my favourite French woman, with love, Victor.'

And then he told her to take her blouse and bra off. There was no changing area or screen in his room so she stripped to the waist with her back to him then turned, trying to relax by closing her eyes.

The breast examination seemed to last an inordinate amount of time. She was thinking how pleasant it was as he massaged and probed her breasts and suddenly she recollected that other doctor all those years ago. Victor seemed to be examining her in the same way, not perfunctorily like other, usually female doctors or nurses. When he finished, she opened her eyes, feeling odd: *This examination seemed rather sensual,* she thought but Victor said, matter-of-factly:

'Everything seems fine. I've put a referral for you on my computer link to the hospital and you should hear direct from them about a mammogram appointment. Then come back and see me again when you have the results.' He grinned at her as she looked over her shoulder at him as she dressed. He was staring at her very intently and then started stroking her back and shoulders.

Clarisse turned to face him. 'And what about paying you? This is a private consultation, isn't it?'

'Don't worry about that; you don't have to pay me anything.'

'Well that's very generous of you, thank you.'

He came over to her, bent down and stroked her cheek. For one micro second she thought he was going to kiss her but he straightened up again.

She blushed and felt very hot, 'It's really stuffy in here. Let's have tea at that café I noticed across the main road.'

*

Clarisse had her mammogram at Colwich Hospital just before the new breast unit opened and received a letter a few weeks later to say the results were negative but that she should have it repeated in a year as there was evidence of calcification. She wasn't sure what this meant so she rang Victor to ask for another appointment as he had suggested but he seemed surprised and said rather abruptly:

'Well, if the results were okay, then there is no need to see me again.'

She didn't think much more about it but he was always so bloody contrary. She thought that he had just wanted to see her again regardless of the results.

They did meet a few more times socially, but after that last strange discussion about him 'changing his life', he had stopped contacting her and if she rang him, he always said he was far too busy to talk. The gossip about him and Grace *and* other women however was rife and it continued to trickle through to her.

*

A few months later, Maggie told Clarisse that the new breast unit was being well received but that Victor was still very depressed, blaming his mental state on what had happened in his private life.

'But maybe he was having a breakdown in any case,' said Clarisse on one of the few occasions they managed to have coffee together after their gym class. 'He behaved very strangely to me, perversely contradictory! And he used to say bizarre things; he told me once he was financing Grace's job so that she wouldn't leave, which is impossible. The hospital would never have allowed it.'

'Men like Victor are very fragile under their magnificent façade.' Maggie paused: 'Emotional distress causes depression, delusion, anxiety, low self-esteem, self-punishment, whatever, and can actually lead to sadism towards others.'

'Well, if you put it in such a didactic fashion, then yes, you could be right. His depressive moods seem to make him act so much less intelligently than he is. He has a brilliant mind but he doesn't always use it to the best of his ability. And all that clap-trap about leaving Faith and him acting so foolishly over Grace.'

Well, he's still with Faith, although he did leave her for a while…'

'Oh, I didn't know that. Where did he go?'

'He either stayed at his office or in some kind of private clinic. And – I have heard that Grace is getting married to someone else…'

'Well, good for her! You know, I have never really understood what makes Victor tick. I tried to be sympathetic but we had a love-hate relationship, well – all hate now – on his part!'

Maggie laughed, saying: 'We have quarrelled too. We're no longer speaking but we've falling out before, but this time I was so annoyed I stepped down as president of the charity. And would you believe it, he's running it HIMSELF!'

'Bloody typical! But, Maggie, you shouldn't let him get his own way with the charity as well. He's unbelievable. How many jobs does that man want?'

'Well, we shall see how he gets on but I still can't dismiss him entirely. His heart's in the right place, you know. He's helped lots of women, including me, overcome breast cancer. He has finally fulfilled his ambition with this fantastic new unit. In the final analysis, it's possible his private life had to be sacrificed for bigger, more important things…'

'Yeah, maybe,' said Clarisse. 'But women today don't just want to be wives, they need wives themselves… while old-fashioned men like Victor want their women to be subservient. I think women are just more *honest* these days and don't play the dumb female so much. We are more confrontational and don't allow men to have their own way all the time…

Women are still disadvantaged, she thought to herself. *It is acceptable for men to have much younger lovers and discard their long-term partners, but then whose fault is this really? Women like Faith shouldn't acquiesce.*

'It's Faith I feel sorry for. We women delude ourselves everything is hunky dory when it is not. But then women will always be attracted to bastards like Victor; we don't like boring men. We like the challenge and can even forgive them their cruelty. It's not just Faith, I know other women, really intelligent women, who stay with men even worse than Victor.'

*

[On board the plane on the first leg of her journey to New Zealand, Clarisse started reading a tabloid newspaper article about an eminent surgeon in East Anglia, who just before retirement had been convicted of rape after a long, successful career in medicine – '…a conspicuous, dashing, sophisticated figure, good-looking, suave, well dressed and not without a certain haughty vanity. Very clever, very handsome and obsessed with sex, he was arrested for drugging and raping a 16-year-old female private patient. Confronted with the forensic evidence he admitted the crime and pleaded guilty without repentance but rather with "amused cynicism". He was diagnosed as being a narcissistic character who considered himself above the law. It had been proved that he

had used injections of iron cobalt (to treat anaemia) on his victim before the rape. Psychologists called as witnesses said he had problems with reality and was bipolar. But his wife was adamant that he didn't have to rape women because he was so successful with them.'

'Surely it can't be Victor?' she asked herself.]

Living in Nettlebury

Dust… and Ashes
Dust to dust and ashes to ashes
There are ashes in the hearth
And dust on the path.
Yet my soul is swept
And my mind is dusted.
Lives are full of chances,
Some defining, some not taken.
Total breakdowns
In communication
And rejections
Make us bewildered.
These hiccoughs
Will be surpassed and
Offence no longer taken.
If we can overcome
Nihilistic negativity,
We can survive – anything.
Anger is a major part
Of the insidiousness, frailty,
Despair and hopelessness
In the difficulty of existence.
We never mean the harm we do,
Our foolish actions
So open to a variety
Of interpretation.
The ash has blown away,
The dust is gone.
Start again, think again, renew.

I will get through this. I promise myself. I am still grieving for Harry but I am surviving. Living on my own is not so difficult. And I don't want people to feel sorry for me. I realise now that I have constructed this hard glacial exterior, that I am unsympathetic. I had a lovely life before Harry died. I feel so empty, so despairing, why should I want to broadcast it?

We are all alone, we all have our own way of coping, I don't want to expose myself... Why should I show my vulnerability...?

People come, people go. I must accept cruel blows, knocks, and criticism.

*

Harry had died because the complications induced by his stroke had been caused by diverticulitis. She had never heard of it but the rather aloof, taciturn consultant at the Nice hospital had explained that when pouches form on the outside of the colon they can become inflamed, causing abdominal cramps. The steroids administered to Harry after the stroke had exacerbated the condition. Harry had complained on and off about tummy pain and constipation but with one thing and another neither of them had ever bothered to register with a doctor in France. They had always been too busy with renovating the house; the wedding; bed and breakfast; working on the theatre and just the novelty of living in a different country. They rarely saw their GP in London when they occasionally returned there and they thought it unfair to exploit the French Health Service. Besides they were both well.

When Clarisse decided to make the move to Nettlebury she continued translating from French to English (as she had done throughout her working life) and volunteered at the Mind charity in Colwich. Financially she wasn't too badly off and received half of Harry's pension as well as some interest from their investments. She enjoyed long walks along the river estuary. Nature was both her consolation and God. The East Anglian landscape was soothing and calm. She didn't miss the intensity of colours and the bright light and heat of Provence. She preferred the more subdued colours of the east coast. The green flatness merging into the grey/blue horizon suited her moods more than the sultry vividness of southern France.

Clarisse took to running along the tow-path of the river estuary. When she ran she felt more grounded, more able to cope with reality and routine. This physical pursuit was spiritually uplifting, like making a pilgrimage. In medieval times a pilgrimage was taken for religious purposes but for Clarisse it satisfied a desire to escape her daily routine and philosophise about her quest to come to terms with life without Harry.

Reading was also a great consolation... Clarisse loved the Occitan literature of the 11th and 12th century, the Provençal poets and troubadours who were the first to express the idea of 'romantic' love. She also admired Christine de Pizan, a Venetian-born medieval author, who is regarded as Europe's first professional woman writer, a feminist who challenged misogyny. Widowed young, she wrote mainly in her adopted tongue of Middle French to earn a living for herself and her three children.

*

Clarisse was making her popular version of paella for her neighbours, Jill and Greg. It was a recipe she had adapted when living in Provence. She still enjoyed cooking, especially for friends. She fried some sliced *chorizo* sausage, took it out and added some chicken thighs to the oil it had made. Then when the thighs were golden she took them out and fried the onion, a garlic clove, half red pepper and one green chilli. She stirred in two cups of *Bahia* rice with a pinch of paprika and a sachet of saffron strands. When the rice was mixed in thoroughly she returned the *chorizo* and chicken to the pan and poured in some chicken stock to cover everything. She then added a few giant prawns but she didn't have any mussels. She added more stock as the rice absorbed it and when it was nearly ready she put a small chopped tomato and a few frozen peas into the pan. Before serving she sprinkled it with freshly chopped parsley and lemon slices.

What she loved about paella was the fact it could all be made in the same large pan.

*

One day when Clarisse was tidying up the flat, she came across some old photos piled up in plastic folders. She started rummaging through them and found a photo of Harry dressed in Elizabethan costume with a beard and wig of white hair. He had been performing in an amateur production directed by his brother James.

'My God, he looks just like Victor!' She had never noticed the similarity between Harry's deep-set dark eyes and those of her erstwhile friend but the beard and the wig made them look identical. She shuddered and stuffed the folder back into the filing cabinet.

*

Clarisse's medical files were mislaid, resulting in quite a long delay before she could have her next mammogram. It finally took place at the new Colwich Breast Unit much later than scheduled. She hated it: the feel cold metal on her flesh; her breasts flattened and pinched under the heavy machine, like slabs of meat held in a vice.

When I had my first mammogram at 50, I was told to check my breasts very often, too often it seemed. The current advice is only to check them every two months and that the best check is still a mammogram. Yet people are now even questioning whether mammograms are a good idea at all…

*

And after two days she received a telephone call: 'The calcification has increased and a tumour has been detected in your right breast. You need to come in as quickly as possible. Can you come tomorrow morning?'

Clarisse took a deep breath, not quite sure if she had really heard correctly. She mumbled 'Yes,' put the phone down and on a whim decided to ring Victor Leach to find out more, even though she hadn't spoken to him for ages. Maybe he could give her some more information about the diagnosis. When she heard his familiar voice she felt more courageous and said:

'Hi, Victor, how are you? It's Clarisse.'

Victor said very coldly:

'I don't want to talk to you ever again.'

'Can't we be friends again and forget what happened in the past? I do need to talk to you as a doctor. I have had some bad news.'

'I don't want to talk to you, even as a doctor. Goodbye Clarisse.'

He slammed the phone down.

She phoned back:

'I need a reason,' but he slammed the phone down again.

She phoned back again.

'I'll carry on ringing until you give me a reason. I've got breast cancer, for goodness sake! I need to talk to you!'

'I'm very sorry to hear that but I don't want to talk to you.'

'Why the hell not?'

'I'm feeling very bad-tempered. I'm a very bad character – and I don't *trust* you any more. Leave me alone, can't you?' He slammed the phone down again.

Clarisse was flabbergasted, her pride in tatters, punctured beyond repair. He had been so cruel.

Clarisse played it over in her mind, wondering what exactly had gone wrong. He obviously blamed her for something... Bloody doctors ...

I suppose this means chemotherapy. All my hair falling out. What's the point? And I can't carry on going to Colwich. I can't see Victor. I must change hospitals... I wish Harry were here, I miss him so much and now this. I suppose there's Gabriel, but he has such strange ideas about women priests. I don't want to see him again. He would be sympathetic but I don't need any God talk. That's the last thing I want. But I must be strong. It happens to all of us at some point. Poor Marion, who died so soon after we became friends again. She developed ovarian cancer even though she'd had a partial hysterectomy. I can't bear to think about how she looked that last week, with all her hair missing after masses of chemotherapy. Marion asked me if she would get better and I replied, 'Yes, of course,' and I rushed out of the room, weeping. The villagers were so mean to her... And poor Guy, he adored Marion, warts and all.

*

The next day Clarisse was examined by Dr Butcher, the oncologist liaising with the histopathology department at Colwich. He told her she would have to undergo either a partial mastectomy or full mastectomy at the special breast unit. She was relieved that Victor was nowhere to be seen and couldn't bear to ask who would be performing the operation. It if wasn't Victor, he would still be in charge and know about it.

How can I have the operation here if Victor is refusing to talk to me?

She thought about writing a letter of complaint, but knowing Victor, he would wriggle out of it somehow –

conjuring up something convincing about her being a difficult patient. And she couldn't be sure that Maggie or anyone else would back her up. There was no one. And she was so tired.

I remember that doctor who touched my breasts; he told me I was prone to breast cancer. That was despicable of him yet maybe he was right all along. If he had just touched my breasts and left it at that, I would have thought him a pervert but would have managed to forget the incident more completely. Yet those words he uttered were indelible. The words were crueller than the molestation. I have always been cosseted and protected; first by my family and then by my darling Harry. I always try to give people the benefit of the doubt. I think human beings are intrinsically neither good nor bad and their behaviour depends on their experiences in life. I'm lucky I've never suffered any traumatic sexual incidents but the memory of that doctor still traumatises me. It's like opening Pandora's Box – I wish all these thoughts would go back inside it box again. I want to close the box – it's all too painful.

*

Although Clarisse had endured a difficult childbirth and undergone several medical examinations she had buried the awful memory from her childhood many layers deep in her consciousness. Going to the doctor or dentist was never a pleasurable experience by any means but it was vital nonetheless. She thought of her body like a car. It had to be serviced and maintained. But now this unpleasant memory had resurfaced and Victor, a supposedly eminent breast surgeon, had also violated her in his way by refusing to speak to her, not caring whether she had cancer or not.

I confided in Victor about that doctor even though I had nagging doubts about the actual experience. After initially being so sympathetic Victor said I could have imagined it. I wonder how many other girls are abused. And how many other doctors are guilty of this kind of behaviour, men who prey on young girls knowing they will do nothing about it? If I had been older and more experienced, I would have been more determined to fight my case against him – even though Mum wasn't keen. I would have tried to get him struck off the medical register.

Women are encouraged to have breast examinations and mammograms but I wonder if some are too frightened to go through the procedure. In spite of this, our health is the most important thing we have and we must put any disturbing experiences behind us. If breast cancer is caught early then the chances of recovery are extremely high. If women don't undergo routine check-ups because they're too scared, then they will be much more scared if they develop cancer and discover it might be too late for treatment. Although... screening doesn't always save lives... It's so complicated.

When I think about how my own experience has affected me, I can't quite gauge how much psychological damage I have actually suffered....

This is a transition. All the anger, frustration, hopelessness, confusion, spitefulness and despair I feel will pass. This is part of the inevitable change from youthfulness and energy to illness and death. From the 'world is my oyster philosophy' to the gradual, reluctant acceptance of growing old. Submission, concession, D E F E A T.

*

Clarisse went to see her GP, Sylvia Leonard, to ask for a transfer to Ipchester. She told her about the mammogram results and Sylvia said:

'I have the letter from Colwich. You need an operation. Haven't you rung them yet?'

Clarisse had met Sylvia a couple of times and found her easy to talk to but she couldn't tell her about Victor.

'I wanted to come and see you first. And actually I would prefer to go to Ipchester. Clarisse didn't agree with the idea of competition in the NHS or the right to choose the best local hospital. Hospitals should be run and financed in such a way that they all attained an equally high standard. Yet she made a feeble excuse: 'A friend told me such good things about Ipchester; her husband received wonderful treatment in A&E and afterwards in the rapid assessment unit. Um – and apparently – there are hygiene issues at Colwich,' she mumbled.

'Well, you are entitled to a transfer if you wish but the breast unit at Colwich has just recently opened – it's state-of-the-art, the staff very professional and efficient. I would recommend you ring them to rearrange your appointment.

'Well, quite frankly, there is one person there who I haven't found very professional. And I really would prefer Ipchester.'

'Okay, fine, I'll contact them now.'

*

At Ipchester she was examined by Dr Chandra. He was young, fresh-faced and chatty. He arranged a series of tests for which she had to stay in overnight. She discovered that he had worked at Colwich with Victor Leach. She tried to ask him what he thought about Victor but he muttered something non-committal and changed the subject. The tests confirmed that the tumour was malignant and that she needed an urgent operation – as soon as a bed became vacant. She would have to undergo either a lumpectomy – a partial mastectomy – or a full mastectomy and afterwards a course of chemotherapy and/or radiotherapy depending on further tests.

*

Clarisse looked up breast cancer on the internet and discovered that its treatment was in the process of being revolutionised, with patients being offered more accurate diagnoses and better-targeted treatments after a study in which scientists genetically mapped the disease. The research found that rather than being a single disease, breast cancer can be classified into ten distinct types. It also identified several new genes that determine the aggressiveness of the cancer. The breakthrough had been hailed by charities as a step towards the 'holy grail' of tailoring treatments to the needs of individual patients.

However there were still conflicting results for drug trials. In future, the new types of cancer drugs would have to be used in combination with older, more successful drugs, but the price was likely to be prohibitive. Treatment would be dictated by financial rather than medical factors.

There was also talk of a vaccine for women with hereditary breast cancer but Clarisse had no history of the disease in her family.

*

I was just starting to cope with life alone, adjusting, surviving the past; functioning in a regular fashion, surmounting mundane tasks, beginning to feel lighter, less burdened but now all is changed. My body is failing; something foreign is growing inside me. I am heavier, pulled down by the weight, the colossus of it all. For a fraction of a second, it's matter over mind. Better to end it all, to slip into oblivion. Assisted death by tranquilliser – take some pills to end it all. No operations or the dreaded chemotherapy...

*

Clarisse did not take fate too seriously and was not convinced that humans are destined to act in a particular way or that lives are predetermined although she now realised that luck did play an important part in life.

I do believe at least that some people are more fortunate than others despite the moral decisions they make. I can be in charge of my own destiny by hastening death and committing suicide. In so doing, I keep control. It's not such a shameful deed as Western civilisation has come to judge. Suicide was considered a noble act in ancient times with Socrates and Lucretius as well as Seneca, amongst others, killing themselves...

Sigmund Freud said that we have a life instinct named 'Eros' and a death drive, referred to as 'Thanatos'. This death drive compels humans to engage in self-destructive acts that could lead to death.

Surviving…

My sea-change
At long last
I shake myself
And see a distant
Light on the horizon.
Abstractions give
Way to reality.
I have so much already.
My intellectual arrogance
So abhorrent to me now.
What right did I have
To think this way
About what
I cannot have
And shouldn't have?
How would a mother
Feel if she loses her son?
Nothing can describe this.
I was so selfish
In my hopelessness
And frustration.
But no matter now.
It is all behind me.
The light is ahead,
I see clearly now.
All is open, no need to lie.

*

Clarisse and her neighbour Jill were sitting on Clarisse's balcony overlooking the Dove River Estuary. Clarisse was drinking green tea but Jill was contentedly sipping the cappuccino she'd made in Clarisse's espresso machine.

Jill and her second husband Greg had a big family between them – five children and ten grandchildren – but she was always interested in other people outside her immediate circle. Like Clarisse, she was a volunteer but worked for a local charity supporting people with learning difficulties.

'When I had my operation in February, Dr Chandra was away and I was told by another doctor that there was no need for further treatment. But after my six-month check-up yesterday, Dr Chandra rang me this morning to say that I have to have daily radiotherapy and at least six cycles of chemotherapy. I'm not sure I want to go through with the chemo. I will talk to Sylvia, my GP, about it all. Marion – my old school friend – had tons of chemo and it didn't help her.'

'Well, it's your decision but if I were you,' Jill reaches over and strokes Clarisse's sleeve, 'I'd go through with it.'

'Do I really want to prolong my life with all these horrid chemicals?' Clarisse sighed. 'We all have to die sometime.'

'But Rissie, it works for other people.'

'Yes, but sometimes the cancer can't be prevented from spreading. Tumours respond in different ways. I would have gone through all that horrible treatment for nothing. Someone I knew at the gym in Aix-en-Provence was killed by the chemo rather than her cancer.'

'Who was that?'

'Her name was Annalise. She lived not far from Potignac. She was the most delightful person, always happy and chatty. And beautiful. She looked like she'd jumped out of a Botticelli painting. Heart-shaped face, gold ringlets, absolutely gorgeous peach complexion, married with three children. The perfect family – but they were besieged by bad luck. Her husband, Gerald, who's a builder, fell off some tall scaffolding and was in a coma for weeks. He did recover and didn't suffer brain damage although he has a metal plate in his head and lost his sense of smell. Not long after, their baby daughter who was born very prematurely caught meningitis and something else, I think. It was touch and go for quite a few months and she had to have several brain operations at the hospital in Toulouse, but she pulled through, thank goodness! She recovered fully and seemed a very lively little girl last time I saw her. But Annalise must have suffered dreadfully – both her husband and daughter so ill within the space of a few months. Then when she was only 39 she was diagnosed with breast cancer. The operation to remove part of her breast and some lymph glands was a success, and while waiting for some breast reconstruction, she was pumped full of chemo. I think she had at least five sessions and she started losing her hair. She bought herself a good wig and carried on her life as best she could. Between sessions she even came to the gym and she and Gerald actually went salsa dancing! Harry and I used to see her regularly at the Potignac market or at church on Sundays. Anyway, the last time we saw her at the market, I told her she was looking really well but she wasn't her usual bubbly self and was complaining about her wig and how hot she felt in it.

'Then on Monday morning we heard the church bells of St Michel tolling. Harry said straight away that someone had died and then took a phone call from a neighbour who said it was Annalise. Eventually we discovered that she'd been taken ill on Saturday evening after picking peaches with a cousin of hers. She'd a very high temperature and was rushed to the hospital in Aix and then her heart gave out. I never really knew the details. Gerald didn't want to take it further but it seems that the high dosages of chemotherapy she was given lowered her immune system so much she couldn't cope with any infection.'

'How terrible – and her poor children! Incidentally, I did read an article about a new gene test being developed to make chemo safer and to eliminate life-threatening side-effects but it'll take about five years to become standard procedure, and only if it's affordable, that is.'

'Too late for Annalise, unfortunately. She was only 40 and so many, many people at her funeral. Her mother-in-law's still looking after the children, as far as I know. Her eldest must be getting on for 18 now, but I don't think Gerald will ever get over it.'

'Such bad luck. Rather like you, Rissie, darling.'

'She was much younger than *me*! I often wonder why life's so unfair but we do have to grin and bear it, take it on the chin and all that. And I've always thought that every individual's cancer and how they react to treatment can be very different.'

'Maybe her husband's accident and her daughter's illness contributed to Annalise's cancer?'

'Very possibly. I think the shock and stress of Harry's death may've caused my cancer too. When I first found out about the cancer, I felt a numbness, I couldn't really take it in, I was too busy trying to erase bad memories about Harry's death.'

'Shock and stress are important factors.'

'And that's one of the reasons I refuse to have any chemotherapy. It can't alleviate a psychological state. And all that pink ribbon stuff irritates me too. Breast cancer isn't glamorous – it's just another disease. Even the rich and famous succumb. Their money can't cure it. We all have to get ill and die sometime. I just have to accept it, not worry about it too much. I don't like showing my vulnerability – I've always wanted control of myself and others, even Harry, but actually it was him directing me, I feel lost without him. But I still don't want to lose control. I don't want being ill to make me spiral out of control…'

It was not the normal conversation one had over coffee.

'Well, you will have to talk to Sylvia about it all. See what she recommends.' Jill continued to stroke her friend's sleeve. 'Maybe you could just have the radiotherapy.'

'She's bound to recommend that I have the chemo as well but I want her to tell me what my other options might be.'

Clarisse finished her remaining green tea.

'If you want me to accompany you to any hospital appointments, I'm happy to drive you there.'

'Thanks, Jill, you're a true friend.'

'Have you told your son about all this?'

'Well, he knows I had the operation. Actually I'm thinking of paying him and Annabel a visit in Auckland – get away from it all for a while. Stop thinking about treatments and maybe travel to the South Island…'

*

After her talk with Sylvia, Clarisse decided what she wanted to do and rang Dr Chandra:

'I'm having the daily radiotherapy and then I'm off to New Zealand for a few weeks' holiday. I definitely don't want to undergo chemotherapy and would prefer alternative treatment if possible.'

'Well, there are new types of less invasive chemo available. They are trialling a cocktail of drugs in London. Ipchester (not Colwich, I hasten to add) has been invited to send cancer patients to Harman Hospital. You could join the trial if you wish. I'll keep you informed…'

He asked her for her email address so that they could keep in touch. She was slightly surprised but gave it to him.

When Clarisse had booked her trip to Auckland for Christmas, Adam her son had been delighted. He and Annabel were expecting their first child and it was due that October so Clarisse would be there after the baby was born.

'Maybe life is not so bad after all,' she mused.

Just before Clarisse left in December Dr Chandra emailed her to say not to forget that various treatments would always be open for her and that he hoped she would change her mind…

*

I don't think I will change my mind. But then again, I might think differently after I get back from New Zealand, after seeing my son and grandchild. I might decide I want to have the chemo to give me the chance to see my grandchild growing up. But then again, maybe I will die anyway and undergoing all that treatment will have been useless. Death could be my final punishment. My terrible guilt brought on my cancer, and now in my despair I don't want to prolong my life. Harry died, so why shouldn't I – quid pro quo? I was taught by the nuns that we have to carry on, come what may, keep a stiff upper lip, be in control, don't crumble, whatever the tragedy. What is wrong with that? I have enjoyed my life, loved food and wine with a passion. But as a counteraction, I have always forced myself to exercise. Any enjoyment has to be counteracted by an opposite discipline. That's how I have conducted my life…

I tried to help others but I'm not sure if I was doing this for them, or rather to fulfil some desire or sense of inadequacy in myself. I have failed; annoyed and irritated too many people. There are several contradictions and failings in my personality, but how else can I be me? Intelligence and beauty and love I have known. Now let me be…

Nostalgie

One person by day, but different at night.
Foreign nuns at school, flapping around
In black and white habits.
Third sex in a coven of witchy females.
Embedded in English education:
Don't cry, don't rush.
Remember: stiff upper lip.
Knuckles rapped if you make a fuss.
At home allowed to love, shout, weep, sleep.
Eat and drink sophisticated fare
Unlike the grey glugs of food at school.
Mum and Dad arguing, then kissing,
Emotions bursting and then all forgotten.
No problem. Yet I don't know who I am.

I enjoyed my life at home in London and never worried about being an only-child. Living in a French household was fun and I liked being fussed over but when I was at school I felt different. When that doctor molested me I was still timid and shy and tried to hide my developing breasts under baggy clothes. I never wore revealing necklines or padded bras and yet I was always agonising about my appearance: trying to straighten my hair, searching for split ends or examining my face for blackheads; experimenting with blue eye make-up.

At the French convent school for girls I attended, there were a few female lay teachers but no male members of staff. I enjoyed the feminine environment. We were taught to be competitive (academically and in sporting events) and there was a great rivalry between our school and the Lycée

Français. And boys – the dreaded 'opposite sex' – were like aliens. I loathed them...

The nuns toughened me up and I became quite cheeky, even aggressive, so much so that by the time I turned sixteen I thought this was the real me. I acted and spoke like the new self, without realising that the other self was still there, so deeply hidden away. Only by peeling away the skin of myself, like layers of an onion, can I discover that once shy, sensitive girl. I do so want to be loved and I can't tolerate criticism. I am still the same girl at heart.

Some more adventurous girls in my class, even girls in the third year, such as Marion, Wendy's younger sister, already had boyfriends. I secretly envied them but I wouldn't admit it. I had never been kissed. I wanted to experience a kiss, but it was an abstract idea, rather than a positive longing. The boys I met were either too juvenile and spotty or too tall and gangly. Besides my parents thought I was too young – 'There's plenty of time for that kind of thing later,' they said.

Some people commented that my mum and I were like sisters. What a cheek! Delphine was at least 30 when I was born. She had brown curly hair like me but as her hair turned grey, she had it tinted golden blonde. She had smooth olive-skin, hazel eyes and a slightly bent nose but my eyes are blue and almond-shaped and I have a small straight nose.

*

The London street where we lived was made up of two terraces of tall four-story Georgian houses with the doctors' surgery situated in the slightly larger end-of-terrace house at one corner of the road. Opposite, on the other corner, was an Anglican church – a mock Gothic monstrosity with a confusion of tall spindly spires and flying buttresses. In later years when property in the area was at a premium and prices were soaring, the church was horizontally divided into two floors and converted into luxury apartments.

I never ventured into this ugly church as the nuns at my school had forbidden it.

'Catholic girls should never go inside a Protestant church. In fact, you should cross the road when you see one.'

This was rather difficult when there was one on the corner of the street where you lived,' I thought, although I never dared to tell the nuns this. But no wonder there is so much animosity between people of different faiths with these ridiculous rules.

At the other corner of the street was a drab, cream-painted and brown-tiled public house called the 'Red Lion' with the usual saloon bar (situated in our road) and public bar (in the adjacent road). Pubs like this weren't fashionable in those days and only heavy drinkers and a few middle-aged, brash, peroxide-blonde women wearing white high-heeled shoes and cheap costume jewellery went there. There was a little off-licence attached to the public bar, where I sometimes went to buy soft drinks and snacks. From the off-licence I couldn't see into the pub, but I could smell it – an invasive combination of beer-damp wooden floorboards and stale tobacco. It made me feel nauseous. Some years later this building too was turned into smart apartments which sold at astronomical prices.

Opposite the pub was a compact Victorian stone-fronted edifice – another church but for Polish Catholics, and dedicated to some unpronounceable Polish saint. Very occasionally I went to mass there when the Roman Catholic service was still recited in Latin; however the priests were all Polish, preaching the sermons in their native tongue. I didn't care as I usually day-dreamed during the sermon, whatever church I was in. I liked the Polish church – the intimate cosy atmosphere, the smell of the candles burning and wax falling

– until the day I went through the main, heavy door of the church, slipped on the torn rush matting and fell flat on my face.

Nevertheless, both Protestants and Catholics had the good fortune to have their spiritual needs – both of the soul and the liquid variety – and their medical needs all catered for in just one small street. It was a shame when the Anglican church and the pub were converted in the property boom. The street lost its symmetry after that, and its notoriety.

*

Clarisse's parents had met during the Second World War. Her paternal grandfather originally came from Toulouse but Eugène Villeneuve was born in London. He was introduced to Delphine Bertaux (known as Dell by her English friends) by one on his relatives in a French patisserie in Soho where Dell was working temporarily, just before he was called up to serve in the British army. They went dancing a couple of times at the Notre Dame church in Leicester Square before it was bombed in 1940. Dell had dreamt of joining the French Resistance but her mother forbade it saying she was too young. Instead she wrote to Eugène and knitted him socks and they married just after the war ended. Eugène's much younger cousin Colette had, however, succeeded in enlisting in the Free French army, lying about her age, and soon after had been shot by the Germans in a reprisal action. Eugène couldn't bear to speak about his cousin and Clarisse never knew the exact details of what had happened to her. In fact Eugène didn't say much about his family at all. The only thing Eugene did tell Clarisse was that he remembered a lovely lady visiting him once. He couldn't really remember her name but thought she was called Raiza and his father, Jacques told him she was Eugène's grandmother. He only saw her once and was later told she died in Italy during the Second World War.

Eugène had started acting at school when he was talent-spotted and cast in a play in a West End theatre with a famous Hollywood actress. It was only a walk-on part but he caught the acting bug and before the war continued to play a few more small roles on the London stage. When he was in the British Army he changed his name to Tony Vines and after the war his agent (whom he met in the army) found him a series of minor comic roles in B-films. With the arrival of television, he had further small roles on the little screen and then quite a long run in a soap opera. When he was 'resting', he worked in French restaurants as a head waiter/sommelier to make ends meet. Eugène often had nightmares about bailiffs banging at the door. At one point he was on the verge of bankruptcy and his excuse had been that his name and account had been stolen by a fellow actor… It was *Maman* Celeste who had to bail him out.

Clarisse didn't think much about her father being an actor. As far as she was concerned it was a job like anything else. And as he wasn't a famous film star, he didn't seem very glamorous. It meant that he worked odd hours and if he was in a West End play he was out most evenings. She actually preferred his jobs at Madame Prunier or the Caprice as he usually came home loaded with lots of goodies such as *boeuf en croûte*, fillets of veal, saddle of lamb and marzipan-covered fruit gateaux.

Delphine used to make chocolate éclairs with choux pastry while Eugène made *coq au vin* with *pommes boulangère* and he loved *ris de veau* (never '*agneau*'). Clarisse had always loved the sound of sweetbreads, like something out of a fairy tale, but refused to eat them once she knew that they were the thymus or pancreas of the calf. Her parents also made *pommes dauphine* – crisp potato puffs made by mixing mashed potatoes with savoury choux pastry. Clarisse often used the same recipe.

*

Delphine Bertaux moved to London in the late 30s to find work and learn English. When her father died, Delphine inherited part of her family's farm in Potignac. She sold her share to a cousin at what seemed like an enormous sum at the time (yet later Clarisse learnt that it went for a song) and with the money Delphine and Eugène bought the Georgian house in North London. Delphine's mother, the widowed Celeste, moved from France to live with them. When her parents died, most of the proceeds from the sale of the house were subsequently used by Clarisse and Harry to pay off their mortgage on their London home, and renovate the house in Potignac. The remainder was invested.

*

Clarisse reminisced about her life in France:

Having been brought up in cosmopolitan London, living in Potignac was initially difficult for me and very different to my memories of summer holidays spent there. I remember the festivals, meeting other young people and enjoying outdoor pursuits; not this herd of gossipy and petty villagers, constantly grumbling.

I was very irritated by the local dialect and the villagers were reluctant to speak standard French. I felt cocooned in the village, where everything seemed unchanging and stuck in time. Yet conversely, although I loathed the conservatism and petite-bourgeois attitudes of the other villagers, this was precisely part of its charm. Nothing has been allowed to change for many centuries in this rural 'paradise' and that's what makes it so special.

I miss my Potignac friends too. Poor dear Marion. She was such fun and she died so suddenly, so tragically. And her poor sister, Wendy, who was in my class at school. I heard that she died about eighteen months later of breast cancer. Their mother too had died of ovarian cancer but Marion didn't always have her regular check-up. Cancer definitely runs in families, like suicide… That's why it's good news that a vaccine might be developed…

And darling Isabelle, a lovely girl and such a talented painter. She wanted to paint Harry's portrait but never got round to it and now it's too late. But life is like this, we don't always keep in contact with our friends, and we don't always have the opportunity to fulfil our dreams…

*

Isabelle had emailed to invite Clarisse to her new show in Lyons. She was finally showing the portrait of that conductor she had been so infatuated with but Clarisse decided she didn't want to go back to France just yet. She was pleased she had managed to rent out the house in Potignac so easily. It was a weight off her shoulders and the small amount of income was a nice little extra but she still felt so guilty about not being with Harry when he died. She had received several emails from Alain expressing his concern about her. She ignored all of them, then one day in her Nettlebury flat she emailed him giving him a brief account of Harry's death and ending it: 'I wished I had never agreed to meet you in Nice.' And never wrote to him ever again.

*

People don't start out evil, we don't commit sins or become criminals deliberately; we act without thinking. Then we try and justify ourselves but mostly our actions are carried out on a whim, or while in a mad mood or temper – 'crimes passionnels' – as they say in French. It is the arrogant individual who deliberately manipulates laws or commits crimes, usually the rich and the powerful, with exceptionally evil motives. The human mind is very unpredictable; we say and do things without thinking of the consequences. Our behaviour is ambiguous, nothing is simple. I think I am good but I can be spiteful. Our thought processes don't always lead to good actions: we want to hurt people and criticise them. We must be good-humoured about life, not take things too seriously. We can be sardonic or sarcastic but without being too cutting or cruel.

*

She thought of her friend Beatrice's flat near Antibes. It was a small studio flat overlooking the bay and Harry and she had both loved it. They usually went out of season – in May or September – before or after it got too hot and crowded. Beatrice was delighted to let them use it as it was empty most of the time and too small to be a viable let.

Clarisse thought the modern little marina quite charming, an artificially created port, full of shops and restaurants where they ate most evenings. And every morning they ran along the beach, over the creek and then along the promenade in the direction of Nice. Running on sand, so different to concrete, feeling the sea breeze and hot sun on her face… Sometimes they drove or walked along the beach to Antibes. She thought of Monet's painting of Antibes in the Courtauld Gallery on the Strand. One of her favourite collections but it had saddened her when the collection had left Woburn Square…

*

'I have such nostalgia for my life in France with Harry. We had such fun living there. His 60th birthday party was wonderful,' said Clarisse to her friend Jill over supper. 'And now I'm thinking of selling the property there. I have no plans to live there on my own.'

'Oh, that would be a shame,' said Jill. 'You might change your mind one day, and what about Adam?'

'Well, living in New Zealand, it's not that easy to get to the South of France and he wouldn't have time to maintain the property. I think he would prefer to come here.'

*

Memories are strange. Some you can relive over and over again until you are unsure if you are only remembering the memories of a memory. My happy memories are a way of assuaging my grief. Other times you want to forget them, pretend they didn't happen. Deleting bad memories can be a normal response to a tragic loss. Like the instant crash of a guillotine, we have the power to curtail memories and crush them completely.

I recall the magical occasion of Harry's 60th birthday party, held on a starry, moonlit, summer night, enhanced by solar lights and flickering candles and the lively sounds of folk musicians. I can still savour the evening smells and the delicious food and wine. Almost like the party in one of my favourite novels, Le Grand Meaulnes, describing that idealised period between adolescence and adulthood; something which is so fleeting and precious that it must be fixed in memory...

Back at the Glass Café

Everlasting eternity
To spend forever
Dancing a dance,
Playing the piano
Or digging a hole.
Immortality inconceivable
When the signs
Of ageing are inescapable.
Every day looking at myself
In an infinity of mirrors,
Smiling at my laughter lines,
Wincing yet
Accepting any wrinkles.
Infinity, purely mathematical:
Watching a play within a play...
Or writing a book about a writer
Writing a book...
Too much to absorb
For the inadequate brain.
Flirting with death,
Relishing an end
That is definite
And with no twist.
Not spiralling into an afterlife
Filled with people I disdain.
Thanking the non-existent Gods
That for me there is no
Eternity, immortality, infinity...

'I don't want to die,' said Clarisse, jangling her large array of gold, silver and bone bracelets on her wrist.

'Well none of us does, darling,' said Jill.

'I *mean* at this stage of my life, but I'm not frightened of dying.'

They were sitting in the Glass Café where she had met Gabriel that time. Clarisse had grown to like this slightly wacky, weather-boarded glass café on stilts. They were at a secluded table overlooking the salt marsh at low tide. The busy docks at Sturwich were looming on the horizon on the other side.

Clarisse certainly enjoyed Jill's company. She was a tonic.

'I love your black and white dress – so elegant, Courrèges, isn't it?

'Yes, vintage!'

'And your curls look so shiny today.'

'My hairdresser's idea – not mine! What I mean is we all have to face death at some point. Look it in the face and not be too surprised when it comes knocking at the door. There's this cult of death in Mediterranean countries. People don't like discussing cancer or dying but once someone does die, a trip to their grave at regular intervals is *de rigueur*. Both my parents hated all that and asked to be cremated. So did Harry. I'm so pleased his ashes are scattered on the salt marsh, it would have pleased him.'

'Yes, it's a lovely spot...'

'Most of us, unless we're suicidal, don't choose when we die or how we die but I'm prepared. I don't want to endure a long lingering illness so I hope the doctors give me something – If I can trust them to put my life – or death, I should say, in their hands...'

'Well, pain management's very sophisticated these days.'

'Yes, I want to be made comfortable. And I believe in DNR – 'Do Not Resuscitate' and die before suffering too much or losing my dignity. I should check out the hospice in Colwich or I suppose I could always go to Dignitas in Switzerland.'

'I'd come with you, if you wanted me to… But hopefully, if the NHS survives, everyone, not just the lucky or wealthy, will have some say when the time comes.'

'Well, if euthanasia was made legal, think how much money they'd save on us oldies…'

'Yes, the present argument is that the NHS can't survive because there are too many elderly patients now. But I bet even in the unlikely event euthanasia is introduced, that would be hit and miss as well. And if the NHS is totally privatised, it'll depend on where you live and what services hospitals offer. This bloody government!'

'Yes, all these cuts are coming at the completely wrong time. When I think what's happening with charities and community care, it makes me want to stop volunteering in protest.'

'I won't be working for 'Mind' when I return from my trip. I do find it so exhausting now. I will content myself with being a 'clickivist' or an 'armchair activist' as I prefer to be called. I'm always signing endless petitions and writing letters these days. I hate those posh, smug boys: Cameron, Osborne and Clegg. They make me so angry!'

'They really don't know how to run the country, that's for sure. Not only are their economic policies flawed but the disabled and the poor are suffering unfairly whilst the rich have their taxes reduced …'

'Anyway, I'm keeping my fingers crossed that euthanasia or assisted suicide, which I believe, is the preferred term, will be legalised here one day too, regardless of party politics,' said Clarisse.

She paused:

'And I certainly wouldn't want to live forever. That would be awful. Immortality is overrated. I want a finite end. Eternal life would be a punishment, not a pleasure.'

'Rissie, you're so brave even to think of these things,' Jill said, squeezing her friend's shoulder.

'Um, I have to confront reality. Be prepared and all that. I know it's rather premature. Cancer isn't always a killer these days. But I don't want to sweep death under the carpet and not think about it. When Harry died I tried to forget what happened, but it's different for me. I don't want to be surprised or scared by it. After all, not one of us knows if we we'll live beyond today. Anyone could be killed by an out of control car or bus, a natural disaster or a freak accident. We don't all die of terminal illness.'

'And you've decided once and for all not to have the chemotherapy?'

'Definitely. As I said, I want to go to New Zealand, visit Adam, and forget about it for a while.'

'But, Rissie, now the cancer's returned, what if it spreads?'

'I've gone over it again and again and I really can't see any benefits. Some people survive, others don't. I don't really believe in destiny but maybe we all have our allotted time; it's either written in our DNA or in the big book in the sky, except I don't believe in that stuff. Religions do fascinate me but they don't provide any answers.'

*

Religion hasn't worked: it still engenders corruption, violence, wars and vice. Anti-Semite, anti-Islam and anti-Christian sentiments are still encouraged. It's an excuse, a fall-back for the fallen; battles fought in the name of religions are an oxymoronic nonsense. The greedy Vatican bank, the

ridiculous Pope and of course, Hitler: he justified his fight for
the German people against Jews by using religion.
*

'You never go to church any more?'

'No, it doesn't mean anything to me.'

'When will you have your next check-up?'

'Quite soon after I'm back from my trip.'

'Will you see the doctor who did the operation?'

'Dr Chandra? No, I don't think so. It's always someone new. You know I've never had much faith in doctors, ever since adolescence. I've met some rather peculiar medics in my time and they always tell you something different.'

'But you did like Dr Chandra?'

'Yes, he was refreshingly honest and open. But he really tried to persuade me to have the chemo. He said I should email him from New Zealand if I had a change of heart!'

'There're evidence-based, new techniques these days but it does depend on your doctor, where you live, and personal circumstances.'

'Dr Chandra did say they were trialling a new cocktail of drugs in London. Or that I could have the routine chemo treatment with injections at home if I preferred, or even an electronic pump, but it's not that. It's what goes into your blood and the rogue effect it can have on healthy cells I don't like. All those chemicals making your hair and nails fall out, weakening your immune system.'

'I've a friend who's a nurse and I related your story about your friend in France to her. She said it's not that uncommon and she always refers to chemo as poison.'

'I'm not surprised.'

'Well, I do understand your point of view. But you might change your mind, you never know.'

Jill said, patting Clarisse's hand.

'Um, I just want to think about my trip. I'm so looking forward to meeting baby Delphine: named for my mother. Adam adored her. She virtually brought him up. Bottle-fed him; made his meals; taught him to read and write; telling him stories. I can still hear her *'Elves and the Shoemaker'*, playing all the parts with different accents. The wife saying, 'Hans, Hans, what shall we do? So many shoes to sew…''

'Your mother sounds a character.'

'She was. And when I die, Delphine will be advancing my mother's and my genes for future generations…'

'Yes, I know what you mean. Sometimes my numerous grandchildren can be little terrors but they're our continuation. That does still give me a thrill.'

'I was slightly miffed Delphine wasn't called after me. Her middle name's Susanna, after Annabel's maternal grandmother.

'D'you think you'll get on with Annabel, staying all that time with them?'

'Yes, I'm sure I will. She's always been very pleasant and she'll appreciate help with the baby. I'm sure we won't argue!'

'No, Rissie, I can't imagine you arguing with anybody!'

'It's funny, I was thinking only the other day, the only person I ever argued with was Harry and I do so miss all that. I haven't got anyone to row with any more!'

'Aha! I'm going to miss *you*, Rissie! If I don't see you before you leave, have a fantastic time.'

'Thanks, Jill.'

They embraced warmly and Clarisse gave Jill her customary three kisses, French style.

Clarisse returned to her meticulously tidy flat, opened the double window to the balcony and walked outside. The bright gold afternoon sun was a retreating line in the layered pink-purple sky. It was low tide and the river glistened as the waters seeped away from the mud flats and patchy, dusky light. On the horizon she could see harbour cranes and a big container ship. She breathed in the salty air and surrendered to solipsistic thoughts.

No longer in charge of my own destiny. Once I never had a sense of self, now I'm too aware of this multi-faceted sullen, surprising, sensitive me. Too egotistical, conscious of every ache or twinge and every blemish. Irritated by that puckered skin hanging from my underarms, mottled, wobbling thighs and disfigured breast.

*

That evening, Clarisse cooked *fusill*i pasta and mange tout peas with a little green chilli and red pepper plus shavings of pecorino cheese and chopped mint and basil. She poured herself a big glass of red wine, pleased she was making proper meals for herself these days. After Harry died, she couldn't be bothered and ate cheese or salad or whatever was in the fridge. Now she conjured up recipes from fresh or seasonal ingredients. Tomorrow she would try that baked salmon dish she made in France, served on a bed of sautéed leeks, fennel and onion and a little crème fraiche. She had lost considerable weight but at least she hadn't lost her appetite.

She turned on the television and watched 'The Merchant of Venice' with Al Pacino playing Shylock, then went to bed but she was restless and couldn't sleep. She lay wide awake, thinking:

Am I in charge? I refused chemo. Will that accelerate my death? While we still have language to express our thoughts and as long as we still have choices and aren't befuddled by Alzheimer's, most of us will want to live. Yet does destiny intervene? In the Merchant of Venice, Portia's suitors have to choose the box containing her portrait in order to win her hand. The man she loves, Bassanio, picks the lead box which is the right choice ... Was this luck or was his character predestined to pick it?

My mother used to tell me that story about Rose-White and Rose-Red. The good little girl called Rose-White fell down a well and found herself in a beautiful meadow. She came across a baker's oven full of bread, and the loaves cried out to her, 'Take us out, take us out! We shall burn, we shall burn.' So she shovelled them all out and laid them in rows.

Then she came to a tree full of apples. 'Shake me, shake me,' cried the tree; 'my apples are all ripe.' So she shook the tree and all the apples tumbled down. Then she carefully stacked them up.

She walked on and found an enormous woolly sheep. 'Shear me, shear me,' said the sheep, 'I have too much wool.' So she sheared the sheep and heaped up all the wool.

Then she came to a little house and an old woman asked her to clean the house. Rose-White swept and dusted, tidied and polished and soon the house was spick and span. The old woman was so pleased she offered Rose-White a choice of two boxes: one blue and one red. Rose-White chose the blue box and to her delight, it was filled with gold and silver and precious jewels. The old woman said she could take the box as a reward for helping her. Rose-Red also went down the well hoping for treasure, but she refused to help anyone. She chose the red box full of snakes, scorpions and spiders... Did the old woman predetermine this and why should blue be better than red? My mother was dyed-in-the-wool, true blue Tory and always dressed me in blue. So for her, did blue signify good and red signify bad? I never asked her. We can lead good lives, make the right choices yet still be unlucky, or like Rose-Red, choose the wrong box and still have been fortunate. Destiny might play a part in our lives regardless of whether we're good or bad...

I can't imagine why the blue box should have been any better than the red box, other than for personal preference or political significance. When I was a child, little girls were not universally dressed in pink as they are now and blue was my mother's favourite colour. The moral of the story my mother wished to reinforce was that industriousness is rewarded. Traditional fairy stories do provide a moral grounding but even after I tried making the right moral choices, life is still unfair...

*

There was a sudden fall of snow. Clarisse enjoyed crunching her way along the river bank in the crispy snow before it turned to slush. Walking in the snow was a struggle, a bit like life really, but she was purposeful: each slow snow-step determined and satisfying. Confronting any obstacle...

Even though people still believe in a 'God' entity the world certainly has not been enhanced and a 'God' or 'Gods' cannot alleviate wrong-doing, general immorality, suffering or death. The spread of cancer may depend on an individual's genetic make-up or psychological state. And my psychological state is baffling me. Being with Alain in Nice when Harry died fills me with self-disgust. Then imagining a priest like Gabriel might be a good friend was foolish and involving myself with the impossible Victor... My pathetic interest in unsuitable men, like a female Orlando Furioso pursuing Angelica is inexplicable and very puzzling, Maybe cancer is my punishment... I was happy with Harry, happy with life in France... I regret my mistakes, my spitefulness and my interferences...

*

As she walked, Clarisse was reflecting that she needed a new accountant and help with her investments which weren't making much interest. Before Harry died, they'd sold their London house and with the proceeds had bought the converted flat in one of the old malt stores in Nettlebury, quite close to where Harry and his brother James had grown up – an always cherished area. It was still a small working port and housed a large malt-producing company. This had resulted in an ever-multiplying swan population that fed off the malt residues pouring into the river estuary from the Maltings.

The odours wafting from the factory varied immensely from the acrid and pungent to a rather inky smell reminiscent of her childhood. Clarisse had grown to love this combination of industry and river life and she inhaled the air deeply.

When Dogs Ran Wild

Questions:
To be honest
With me and others.
Cheating, Stealing,
Extortion, Corruption:
Necessary
Facts of Life?
Easy or easier
To tell the truth?
Say what we mean
Humbly,
So less corruptible
By snaky
Sharks…

Thankfully it was just a dream. Denys woke up, sweat pouring down his pyjama-clad chest, his legs tangled in his tousled sheets. He'd dreamt that his Ming china was lying on the beige carpet shattered into hundreds of tiny pieces. He'd been fumbling with his pistol, not quite sure how to get his finger round the tiny trigger and had accidentally fired at the custom-made maple cabinet containing his prized collection of 15th century blue and white vases. The only things he had ever really loved.

*

There was something insubstantial about Denys Phillips as if the threads of his personality hadn't quite woven together. The word 'phlegmatic' sprang to Clarisse's mind. He was two-dimensional; making all the correct responses when she spoke to him but never engaging in any meaningful conversation.

Clarisse knew of him through Nancy, who had been married to Harry's elder brother, James. They had endured a bitterly contested divorce but Clarisse had kept in touch with her ex-sister-in-law periodically. When James and she were still together they had bought a place in Dordogne or 'Dordogneshire' as Harry called it. Harry was dismayed when he learnt that Nancy, whom he detested, was living on French soil, but they'd only ever been to their house once and Harry vowed never to return as 'Nasty Nancy behaved so rudely.'

Soon after, James ran off with one of his fine-art students at the exclusive six-form college in Oxford where he taught. He kept the place in France as part of the divorce settlement and Nancy retreated to Hertfordshire.

Harry had been relieved to sever all contact with 'Nasty Nancy' but Clarisse still heard from her occasionally. When Harry died James had been exceptionally helpful sorting out Harry's cremation in France and assisting Clarisse in the difficult task of getting his ashes through French customs. Nancy had insisted on attending Harry's memorial service in Nettlebury, much to James's annoyance, but Clarisse hadn't liked to discourage her. Nancy was with her new partner, Julian March, her old creative writing teacher. Julian was very proud of the fact that he 'had never learnt to swim'.

Odd chap, so drab and undistinguished, not like the two dashing brothers, James and Harry, Clarisse thought.

Nancy favourite words were 'awesome' and 'gruesome'. She told Clarisse that she was writing a 'gruesome' thriller about serial killer…

'How thrilling,' retorted Clarisse.

*

When Clarisse returned permanently to England she'd stopped using her accountant. He too had a house in France –

that's how they'd met – but he was becoming too expensive and when Nancy recommended Denys, married to her sister, Ruby, Clarisse seized the chance as she thought it would be too tiresome finding anyone else.

Clarisse met Denys for the first time when she handed over her tax files to him in North Hill. All she knew about him was that he had worked in Canada briefly before moving back to England and marrying Ruby. Denys had been very reassuring:

'Don't worry, Mrs Villeneuve, I'll take care of your tax return and the rebate owed to your late husband plus your investments; all for a modest fee!' Before being ushered into Denys's office, Clarisse had chatted briefly to Ruby in the house, mainly about Nancy: 'Well, she's a published author now and very high and mighty!' said Ruby.

'Oh, I'll have to ask her for her autograph next time I see her!' said Clarisse, laughing.

The décor was dreary beige with the exception of an enormous, black, flat-screened television. Clarisse had noticed the Ming china displayed in a brown cabinet but it looked lustreless in its undistinguished surroundings and as dull as its owner.

His annexe office, a minimalist white box room with additional white loo and galley kitchen – solely used for making coffee – was where Denys spent most of his time. Apart from his Ming collection, Denys had never indulged in collecting paintings or other ornaments so only his files were displayed. Occasionally he fingered what he called his 'toy' in its secret draw.

*

Denys wasn't one for self-analysis or introspection. He voted Conservative, just as every good accountant should. He was of average intelligence although his large head suggested otherwise. He had started losing his hair in his twenties so he shaved his head, making him resemble a shiny, soft, pink egg or 'Humpty Dumpty' as his former colleagues secretly referred to him. His face was round and oily. His eyes were an indeterminate brown under reptilian eyelids, surrounded by barely visible eyelashes and sparse blonde eyebrows. Clarisse thought that if endowed with few attractive physical features, people made up for it in personality but Denys was lacking in both; yet happily oblivious to how other people perceived him.

Denys didn't go to university but studied accountancy at a highly reputable firm. After qualifying as a chartered accountant, he worked for a steel works in Humberside. Then, on a whim, he applied for a job at a Canadian firm of accountants called Bragg & Bragg in Worthington, Ontario, advertised in the Times. He was flown over for the interview and was offered the job on the spot. 'This is,' he thought, 'the best moment of my life'. The salary was twice his existing one so he was delighted to leave nuts and bolts behind him. He was given a grace-and-favour apartment in the nearby town of Gouda. Most of his fellow accountants came from overseas like himself. He soon discovered that his clients were businessmen who had emigrated from Campania or Sicily with French-Canadian mafia connections. Occasionally Denys accompanied the most important 'bosses' to New York in a black, bullet-proof, smoked glass, stretch limousine and Denys was extremely uneasy at witnessing unsavoury deals on some thirty-something-floor of some dazzling glass and steel skyscraper on the Manhattan skyline. Most of these stereotypically dark, overweight men carried guns in hidden holsters under their expensively tailored black suit jackets. On a solo trip to New Jersey, after advice from a colleague, Denys walked into a gun shop, purchased a licence and a very small silver pistol. It looked like a toy.

Mingling with the 'underworld' made Denys uncomfortable and he perspired even more profusely: 'What have I got myself into?' he often wondered yet he was strangely drawn to them. Consorting with criminals gave him a secret thrill. Theirs was an alien, hostile world, so unlike his former lower-middle class existence where his only hobbies had been train-spotting or noting down unusual car number plates. He succeeded in gaining his clients' respect and the partners in the firm were so pleased with his precise and methodical, if 'unethical' tax avoidance work, his salary was increased to an extraordinary figure. He was encouraged to buy a penthouse in down-town Worthington by the top boss, Mr Carducci. Worthington was an unspectacular, comatose little town built on a grid with row upon row of neat and uniform suburban housing, mainly bungalows, each with spacious yard and double garage surrounded on three sides by bleak expanses of industrial parks. Denys could walk to the Bragg offices situated in the main street; the only lively street in town. Denys was the only employee to walk to work as most of his colleagues had families and lived in the suburbs; or were just too lazy not to use their expensive, showy cars.

Denys needed a distraction and became fascinated by Ming porcelain. He gathered together a rather impressive collection but he was too nervous to enjoy it, constantly looking over his shoulder, thinking he might get gunned down at any minute. He was comforted by the presence of the little pistol hidden in his desk. Sometimes he got it out and held it in his clammy fingers. He rarely socialised and stayed inside his apartment, ordering take-out food or making himself starchy snacks. He was therefore delighted to be sent on a trip to Hong Kong, hoping for once the Mafia wasn't involved; but unbeknownst to him the client was a Triad with links to his French clients. While he was eating alone one evening at a fifth-story Korean restaurant on Kowloon, he struck up a conversation with a young woman sitting at the adjacent table. She was Anglo-Chinese and Denys found her very personable. He introduced himself and discovered her name was Ruby. Although diffident at first, she was a good listener. Denys usually kept things to himself and it was with a certain relief that he confided in her:

'I earn a very good salary in Canada but the company I work for is rather shady and I really want to return home to England.'

Ruby became more animated. Denys wasn't attractive but he was English *and* an accountant. 'Well, my sister Nancy married an Englishman.' She didn't mention the divorce.

'They have a house in France and Nancy's started writing. She's working on a thriller, something about mushroom poisoning.' Ruby said in a dismissive tone. Secretly, she had been eternally envious of her elder sister. 'I've always wanted to work in England. Maybe we could get jobs there at the same time,' she said.

'I'd need to give the firm six months' notice. Strange thing is all the time I've been there no one's left, but I'm desperate.'

'Well, you've got plenty of time to find work then.'

Ruby was a psychology graduate, in between jobs and anxious to get on in life. She thought marrying someone like Denys, in spite of his looks was an attractive proposition – *and* he was quite tall!

Denys succeeded in finding a job at a software company in North London and urged on by Ruby, he quitted Bragg & Bragg without working his full notice period. The top boss, Mr Carducci, smoking his perennial cigar, was livid:

'Mr Phillips, you're leaving under a big, fat cloud. Some clients gonna be very unhappy at your departure. You have some very damaging, sensitive, even sensational information about them. I thought you had more loyalty to Bragg's.

You've betrayed our trust – you might live to regret this. I'm very disappointed, Mr Phillips.'

Denys was made to sign a non-disclosure agreement with Carducci demanding he leave the building immediately, giving him very little time to gather up his few personal possessions. The next day he put his apartment up for sale with the local real estate agents; carefully packed up his Ming porcelain (with his pistol wrapped in tissue paper and hidden inside one vase) and certain large items of furniture for shipment to England and purchased an extremely expensive ticket to Heathrow on the next available flight.

'I'm safe at last,' he thought, clutching the arms of his seat and closing his eyes. Even the terrible turbulence didn't disturb the first deep sleep he had enjoyed since he left England.

Denys and Ruby continued their 'whirlwind' romance by telephone and email between London and Hong Kong. He organised and paid for her trip to Heathrow, even bought her a winter coat. They got married in Watford Registry Office with his parents as witnesses who were delighted Denys had finally settled down. They could cease worrying about their only child. Denys had never encouraged a visit to Canada so they were relieved that he was back on home territory.

Denys made a tidy sum for his Worthington penthouse and together with his savings from his substantial salary, bought outright a two-bedroom bungalow near where his parents lived. He furnished it with Canadian items and his beloved Ming, which arrived in record time and all intact. As he placed the china very carefully in a specially designed Canadian maple cabinet he thought how well it looked in its new English home. His only happy memories of his sojourn overseas were buying the Ming from a Chinese-Canadian dealer. His favourite was the blue and white 17th century fruit bowl decorated with deer and cranes. The dealer had said it had been found in Pavilion of Moral Obligations from the Forbidden Palace in Beijing. Unfortunately it had a hair-line crack, but was still worth a considerable amount of money.

He methodically unpacked his other belongings and tucked away some accountancy books and personal files together with his little pistol in the desk drawers in his study. He came across a file marked 'Confidential' with a thick white foolscap envelope inside it. He pushed it to the back of a drawer, not having the time or inclination to identify the mysterious document; too preoccupied about Ruby who was arriving the next day.

When Ruby saw the bungalow, she said: 'Oh, Denys, it's so small!' However she quickly adjusted to England, got temporary work at a secretarial agency and determinedly set her heart on a bigger, better house in North Hill, the most prestigious neighbourhood in the county.

After two years at the North London company, the economic climate was ideal for Denys to set up his own practice which he baptised 'Macmillan'. It wasn't difficult for him to drum up custom from the contacts he had made in previous jobs (apart, of course, from Canada). His clients didn't mind his blandness. As long as he balanced their books and discovered tax-loopholes, his clients remained content. Gradually his client-base swelled, mainly with word-of-mouth recommendations. He also gained useful connections in Hong Kong, as the formidable Ruby was very adept at getting his name passed around amongst former friends, colleagues and her large family; some of whom had business interests in Europe. Denys soon earned the reputation for being dependable and an 'honest accountant'. Within a year they moved to the house of Ruby's dreams in North Hill: a large, detached, red-brick mock Georgian affair set in large gardens on a tree-lined avenue filled with similar properties. Denys had an annexe office specially built on one side to match the double garage on the other. Soon, Ruby gave birth to Graham, who resembled his mother. Ruby wasn't beautiful but she had regular features and thick glossy blue-black hair. Graham grew into a beautiful boy and started prep school. Ruby persuaded him to take up rugby, cricket, martial arts, violin and piano at a tender age. Denys was not particularly involved with his upbringing and it was Ruby who directed filial operations.

Things were going so well that Denys hired an assistant and bought himself a new Jaguar *and* a Range Rover for Ruby to carry Graham to his various activities. Denys was keen to give Graham every possible advantage: 'I want him to have all the things I couldn't,' he said whenever Ruby suggested any new plan for their son.

Then Denys was badly affected by the Lehman Brothers Bank collapse which shook the global markets. With the absence of any new clients he had started giving financial advice to existing ones, urging them to invest in schemes purely because he received enormous commissions for them. He then started an affair with his assistant, Sharita. He said: 'Ruby's so distant these days, I can't tell her anything now, unlike you, Sharita, you're so understanding.'

Recently Denys's thoughts had returned to Bragg & Bragg. 'I bet they haven't been affected by the markets.' In a rare moment of honesty he suddenly realised that he envied Mr Carducci and his empire – all that power and testosterone swagger. He missed that atmosphere of male dominance he had encountered in Canada, even the ever-present threat of violence. He had been subdued by Ruby, not by Bragg & Bragg after all.

When they could manage it Denys and Sharita went on 'business' trips to the West Country. Not long after, he inexplicably lost two major English clients and others in Hong Kong followed suit. To make matters worse his personal investments were wiped out in the sub-prime crisis. He had bought into an American mortgage brokers, seemingly a good investment, but as events proved, it was unsustainable and the profit bubble burst. Denys became increasingly concerned about his financial problems. He didn't dare tell Ruby and when she asked, he said: 'Don't worry, Ruby, everything's going swimmingly!'

He spent many hot, sleepless nights alone, battling his damp sheets. He and Ruby slept in separate bedrooms. It had started when Graham was born and Ruby had suggested sleeping in Graham's room so as not to disturb Denys while she breast-fed at night. Graham was now six and Ruby still shared the same room with him. She said: 'It's only because I can't stand you sweating, Denys!'

Denys was at his wits' end. He owed money everywhere: outstanding payments on the mortgage and cars costing thousands a month. He had stopped making cash purchases and had borrowed up to the hilt.

However Denys wasn't at all concerned with the 'niceties' of life. The family usually ate out once a week but it could be Little Chef for all he cared. In summer they went to Torquay for their fortnightly holiday and every two years visited Ruby's family in Hong Kong, either at Christmas or Easter – always flying business class. Ruby would have guessed something was up if he had changed to economy so he booked Ruby and Graham's next trip to Hong Kong for Christmas. He used the excuse of joining them later – on a cheap economy flight – as he had so much work to finish.

'What can I do, Sharita? I can't really afford to keep you on but Ruby would be suspicious if I fired you and besides, I need you so badly…'

Then to top it all, the property scheme he had recommended to clients such as Clarisse went bankrupt after being officially declared illegal so consequently his commission fees failed to arrive. Sharita comforted him.

'You'll just have to start charging higher rates.'

'But then everyone will stop using me.'

'We'll think of something,' Sharita said, patting his pale pate.'

Perhaps it was time to start acting like Mr Carducci, even in a small way. Denys filled out his clients' self-assessment tax returns on-line, adding their personal bank account details for any tax rebates due from Her Majesty's Revenue and Customs. Now Sharita inserted the Macmillan bank account on all the returns and the proceeds from HMRC were paid directly into this account. Denys informed his clients by email that he had received tax rebates on their behalf and had deducted his fees in advance so most of them only received a tiny proportion of the amount owed.

Unlike Clarisse, some didn't even notice the increase. She was furious as the fee was much higher than his original quote, almost treble in fact. She phoned Denys to query it and he said:

'I've done nothing wrong. Solicitors charge in advance. In fact I've done much more work than I anticipated. I should have charged you even more.' Denys said calmly.

'How can you say that? It was only a tax return! And I was relying on that tax rebate.'

She could almost feel Denys shrugging. He put the phone down and said to himself: 'Stupid woman, I could have fiddled her much more if I wanted to. Maybe I should cream off more from her investments. Bankers are doing it, so can I.'

Clarisse sought advice from various people and was told to lodge a complaint with the Institute of Chartered Accountants but she didn't have the time or energy to pursue it as she was just about to leave for New Zealand. She was subsequently informed about the property company bankruptcy and that she wouldn't receive any compensation. She had to be 'stoical' and not let mere money matters upset her. She'd always disdained material wealth and now it was her health that was most important. However it was a big blow financially and her investments were hardly worth anything. Even so, she still had to think positively…

*

Bloody accountants! I'll fill out my own tax return in future. And when I checked my copy, it had my bank details on it, not his. Damn him! I don't want any more to do with Denys and Ruby, or Nancy for that matter. How could a chartered accountant be so dishonest? These days we're 'morally' flexible; some of us honest, others not. Some precariously close to breaking the law; many even do. Some get away with scams or bad practice, others wouldn't. I couldn't live my life in a moral dilemma – I'd rather commit suicide – but I suspect Denys hasn't got the imagination or inclination to do that. It used to be the honourable thing to do – not now. Maybe I should challenge him to a duel…

And at least I still have the rent from the house in France… Stupid Denys wanted me to sell that too… and would have made even more unwise investments with that money too…

*

As Clarisse was sleeping on the plane from Heathrow to Dubai on her way to Auckland, back in North Hill Ruby was feeding her two pugs, Beano and Topper, when she heard a persistent ringing of the bell.

*

Two stocky men in sunglasses, wearing identical black suits, were at the door.

'I wanna see Denys Phillips,' the more rotund and sinister of the two grunted in a Canadian accent.

'He's in the office on the left'.

They both knocked violently on the white door and Denys opened it himself as Sharita was in the kitchen making coffee. Before he could ask who they were, the scarier stranger said:

'Good mornin', Mr Phillips. It sure has taken me a while to track you down. I want that package you lifted from me more than six years ago.'

'I... I ... don't know what you're talking about,' Denys said, wishing he was back at his desk.

Time stopped still in the icy, wintry silence when two strange, unidentifiable bangs were heard emanating from the office. Ruby flew there to find the door wide open and Denys sprawled on the floor, clutching his bleeding chest. There was no sign of the mysterious hit-men. She hurried back outside and glimpsed a black limousine, tyres crunching gravel, speeding out of the drive. The two pugs waddled out of the house, barking furiously at the retreating vehicle. Their wrinkly, short-muzzled faces creased even more intensely; their curly tails wagging ferociously as they ran as fast as they could out of the drive, wildly but fruitlessly...

New Zealand Journal

To be or not to be – French?
That essence of me at
Home echoing of
Shouts and arguments.
At school more modest, well-behaved,
Softer yet stricter words;
Only thoughts and crosses
To bear, confused.
Death comes or does not.
He loves me, he loves me not.
Cancer's hold on me
Fatal or curable?
My stubborn refusal
To say yes to doses of
Chemotherapy, why not
Depart of my own accord?
Why do people have to conform?
Why do doctors have to be obeyed?
Nature tells me to
Refuse all treatments.
Better to keep my tresses,
My talons, eyebrows, eyelashes.
No venoms to
Course through
My blood rushes…
No floods of tears…
No hot flushes,
No rashes, no crashes.

Tuesday

I'm on the plane and plan to keep a record of my trip in this newly acquired journal. I have also bought myself a fountain pen so my hand-writing will hopefully be more legible. I am so used to tapping away at a keyboard that hand-writing is becoming ever more difficult. But I used to love writing with a proper pen so I hope I can now get back into the habit of it. Jill suggested writing a diary would be therapeutic. I don't profess to be a good writer but I will want to be as honest as I can about my thoughts and feelings in this somewhat unclear stage of my life. I wrote the above attempt at poetry in the departure lounge at Heathrow and have stuck it at the front of this journal. I am not a poet by any means but writing like this helps me and my mood's brighter already and I don't feel so despondent, so lost as before …

I am hoping to find peace…

New Zealand will be a new experience, maybe a new beginning for me… I have decided not to contact Alain. That's all behind me.

Arrived in Dubai later than expected and sat in transit lounge before very late boarding of plane via Sydney to Auckland. Some confusion over seating even though I'd checked-in on-line but got aisle seat in the end. My young neighbours snoring with mouths open. Terrible turbulence and I couldn't sleep so watched a few unmemorable films but must have dosed off because I had horrid dream about Denys! He *did* get his comeuppance! And I woke up with terrible pain in my chest and feeling claustrophobic in the pressurised cabin.

A thought:

People with terminal illnesses could sink into a moral abyss and kill someone they hated, knowing that he/she were going to die anyway. Personally I couldn't kill anyone. I despise Denys for losing me all that money but I don't wish him dead; maybe just metaphorically rapped on the knuckles and 'reformed'. His actions were surprisingly out of character. I always thought he was as genuinely honest as Nancy led me to believe. Now I really must forget about him. What's done is done…

Friday
AUCKLAND
Adam is here
Unflappable, unassuming,
Cool and collected,
King Kiwi,
Lord of the Rings.
And after all, there is
No, certainly, no
Disquietedness between us.

Arrived in Auckland on time. And Adam was in the arrivals lounge waiting to pick me up. I hadn't seen him since Harry's cremation and we kissed awkwardly. He took my suitcase and ushered me to the car park. He now owns a BMW estate. He must be doing well…

Delphine at three months is a delight and so good at night. She sleeps through until 6 in the morning! It's such a joy to see my first grandchild but it's so sad that Harry didn't live to see her too. All that baby sweetness and silkiness; her fresh clean smell; smiling; biting; kicking; tugging, clutching fingers.

Christmas in Auckland
Christmas is the start of the summer holidays. Annabel's family go to their 'bach' (pronounced 'batch'): a traditional holiday dwelling – anything from a large beach hut to a proper house. New Zealand virtually closes down in an almost

enforced 'isolation' when normal routine is disrupted for several weeks. Adam thinks this long holiday highlights the absurdity of a 'Pagan mid-winter festival' transplanted to mid-summer. He says it's when ex-pats realise you live on a small island at the 'arse end of the world' and you have to get your head around traditional Christmas paraphernalia after you've just got back from the beach. Adam and Annabel or AA (as I call them) aren't putting up any decorations – incongruous in their smart, pristine apartment on the Eastern shore. I agree but they're not even getting a Christmas tree. Surely when Delphine's older she'll want to see a tree with lights and decorations and presents under it! I insisted that we have a proper lunch (rather than beach barbecue) and plan to make a special meal for them with Christmas crackers and candles on the table. As a European, I want to keep to the old traditions even though AA would prefer to spend as much time outside as possible. Adam did point out that swimming off a New Year's Day hangover is preferable to watching crap television during a heavy downpour. He wanted us all to go to the beach for a few hours, back in time for a late lunch but I said I would prefer to cook everything while they're at the beach. Weather here can change suddenly, even in summer. Either grey and overcast or as hot as Provence; so all hoping for the latter! Adam warned me the rainfall is almost subtropical and I shouldn't expect wonderful weather on my road trip. Apparently he saw snow once and the Kiwis ran to the office window – most had never seen it before – but it only lasted ten minutes.

Sunday

I cooked *boeuf en croute* and veggies for Christmas lunch, preceded by the oyster and vodka shots Annabel made. Something I've never tried before and most probably will never try again… Then we had *panettone* from their local deli and fruit salad and ice-cream. The fruit's lovely here. We ate on the balcony overlooking the monstrous fountain in the palm courtyard *and* the Pacific. Adam insisted we had a bbq on the beach on Boxing Day. Deliciously warm – and sausages and hamburgers. Stripped down and dabbled my toes in the water but didn't swim as it was freezing! (Adam looked quite shocked when he saw how thin I'd got.) I played with Delphine and AA swam. So good to feel the sun on my skin but not as hot as the Med! On New Year's Eve I baby-sat while AA went to party. I reread Mrs Dalloway, found on their bookshelves, and played Verdi's La Traviata on their complicated CD player.

Adam's helping plan (*dictate*) my journey. He's on holiday but goes to the office occasionally. I play with the baby or help Annabel with the housework. There's always so much washing to do with babies around. I've never really been maternal and hated breast-feeding but I'm in love with Delphine. She's adorable and so pacific. I'm so pleased her parents haven't allowed her a dummy. I stick my little finger in her rosebud mouth and she sucks on it with vigorous enthusiasm… She even enjoys my rendition of Peggy Lee's song about a 'bambino' going to sleep. In evenings, cook for AA, who're both very appreciative. I'm experimenting: combining meats with fruits, such as *canard a l'orange* (obviously) pork and pineapple, chicken and apricots …

Things to see in Auckland – Tāmaki Makaurau
What makes Auckland exceptional is its natural setting and bright light while it's not as imposing as, say Rio de Janeiro. It's built on a volcanic field sandwiched between the Tasman Sea on the west coast (also known as 'The Ditch') and the Pacific to the east. It has over 40 extinct volcanoes, manifest as individual hills and known as 'Pa' after former Maori settlements. We went to two in Devonport (on the

North Shore where one of Adam's friends lives). One's called North Head (full of tunnels and coastal battlements) and the other, Mt Victoria (Takarunga in Māori) with magnificent panorama. Two of Auckland's parks – called domains – are on the side of these volcanoes – Auckland Domain (home of the Imperial War Museum including Maori/Pacific Island history) and Cornwall Park. The main natural landmark is the imposing volcanic island of Rangitoto, off the east coast, visible from much of the city. The harbours, coastline, islands and beaches are Auckland's real jewels. The suburban east coast where AA live has a number of lovely, sheltered beaches – so different to crowded Mediterranean. The west coast is more rugged with the Waitakeres, a marvellous rainforest mountain range. It's full of ferns and damp as a Kew Gardens hot-house. The isolated, wild beaches of Piha (where we went for the day) and Murawai have black volcanic sand – on first glance like oil. There're big, big waves ideal for body boarding and surfing. (Incidentally, Piha is where they filmed Jane Campion's 'The Piano'.) Because of New Zealand's island nature the sea takes a lot of people so it has more than its fair share of drownings.

Drowning wouldn't be a bad way to die… walking into the sea with rocks in pockets. I've always liked the idea of being buried at sea. Back to where it's said life originally derives. My Pantheist ideal… but I don't think AA would be very happy with the mess my suicide would leave behind…

I don't know that many people who have committed suicide. It seems to run in families: that friend of Harry shot himself with a hunting gun and then his father did the same thing on the tenth anniversary of his son's death. And Marion told me about someone in Tooting, an Austrian woman who committed suicide when she was 50. Marion felt so guilty but it turned out the Austrian's mother had committed suicide at the same age. I can't think of anyone in my family committing suicide. I would be the first… a suicide-virgin…

Auckland is composed of a series of Art-Deco style centres, rather than one main centre, with multitudinous theatres, cinema, museums and art galleries. Auckland's only real man-made landmark, the Sky Tower (one of the Southern hemisphere's tallest buildings), can also be seen everywhere. Annabel had vertigo and I wasn't that desperate to go up it! Was supposed to take the ferry to Waiheke island but somehow we didn't, maybe next time!

The cheapest places to eat are the food courts selling mainly Asian food where we went a couple of times. Baby Delphine fell happily asleep on both occasions. The Japanese food was excellent and the second time I had some good vegetarian Indian. One evening we all went to a lovely restaurant overlooking the harbour in the 'Viaduct'. Last Monday Adam helped me climb up Mount Eden (phew!) and on Wednesday we visited Toi o Tāmaki – the Auckland Art Gallery. I liked Rita Angus and the prolific Frances Hodgkins who painted landscapes and still-lives. I admired her chalk drawing of Cassis and a wonderful nude by A Lois White. South Auckland (also known as called Manukau, Maori for 'wading birds') is called the Polynesian city – where all the Pacific Island people (from Samoa, Cook Islands, Fiji, Kiribati and Vanuatu etc.) live. They keep to their island traditions while fully participating in the wider Auckland community. The city has many Pacific Island churches (I saw some Samoans or Tongans in traditional church dress) and various Maori meeting places (called 'Marae').

One evening AA organised babysitter and booked us to see the very good New Zealand Symphony Orchestra – NZSO – in the Town Hall playing Beethoven's 9th.

Thursday

Last night I cooked a final *cassoulet* with duck, Toulouse sausages and flageolet beans, followed by apple pie: my grandmother Celeste's recipe with Calvados cream topping. Greatly appreciated and washed down with delicious Gewürztraminer ….

… Adam's now uncharacteristically worried about my road trip!

My thoughts and feelings still so confused.
Is death coming?
Is my cancer inevitably fatal
If conventional treatment is refused?
What does this say about me?
Stubborn, stupid, selfish?
Yet am so happy to have seen Adam
Here on the other side of the world;
To have been reconciled,
No more awkwardness between us.
He's settled now and has a lovely life.
No need to worry about me.
So will death ring?
Perhaps, who knows?
My instincts tell me to resist.
Is it my destiny to die or to live?

My moods change constantly but it was definitely the right decision to come here. Even if it's my last big trip…

… I plan to drive from Rotorua to Wellington, get ferry to Picton on South Island and head to Christchurch and fly back to Auckland from there. Adam's organised hire of four-wheel-drive Nissan Xtrail. I'm borrowing their car socket-operated cool box and a very large umbrella.

ROTORUA – *first stop on my solo road trip adventure!*
Rot? What rot, nothing rotting, rotten
Or tortuous,

Tormented theodicy
Or
Revolving, rural, rich,
Undemanding, uncomplicated, unsung
Amiable, attractive and amenable.

Rotorua (from the Māori: *Te Rotorua-nui-a-Kahumatamomoe = 'The second great lake of Kahumatamomoe'*) is on the southern shore of Rotorua Lake in the Bay of Plenty. Stayed a couple of nights with my second cousin, Rosemarie and husband, Gordon. Arrived early afternoon after three-hour drive from Auckland. There're no real motorways so the 140-mile stretch took some time but I did digest the scenery and amazed myself by not getting lost. Thankfully Rosemarie gave me very good directions. When Gordon returned from work they gave me tour of the centre and a drive around the blue green lakes. That evening we had a bbq even though it rained! In the morning Rosemarie took me to the Rotorua Museum of Art and History in the old Bathhouse building with bathrooms all still visible. Lovely display of Maori wooden boats, intricate carved doorways and ornaments. Unlike me, Rosemary's very energetic considering she's had a rare blood cancer. She lost all her hair but luckily it's grown back. One of the reasons I hate the idea of chemo is because of the hair loss. I would miss my thick, curly hair. I don't want to be bald! Yesterday evening they took me to a Maori evening at a local hotel with buffet dinner and cabaret. Stuffed myself with green-lipped mussels and crayfish; followed by delicious steamed lamb and a variety of puddings and honeycomb ice-cream. Gordon was hauled up onto the stage for traditional '*haka*' dancing. He had joked in advance that he wasn't keen on audience participation and lo and behold he was chosen! Part of the dance ritual involves the sticking out of tongues. Gordon excelled at this, receiving huge applause from the audience! Ill in the night. Following morning after breakfast I said my goodbyes and drove to volcano park: WAI-O-TAPU THERMAL WONDERLAND. Wai-O-Tapu or 'Sacred Waters'; an active geothermal area in the Taupo Volcanic Zone with many hot, colourful springs. I began by watching the geyser, seated with a crowd of people in a circle, almost like a Roman amphitheatre. Chap directing the show used bar of soap to start it, insisting it was eco-friendly but I was disappointed it had to be started in this way. At first the geyser was just a small jet but it rose up like a huge flame and I could feel the heat of it – 100 c. – from where I was sitting quite a distance away. Then I embarked on circular group walk to the various craters and pools. My favourite was the Artist's Palette, a combination of greens, oranges and yellows. Very psychedelic! Then onto to the Champagne Pool with its large creamy surface. It looks like liquid but it's molten rock. The other geysers were called Lady Knox and Primrose Terrace. Finally I went to the boiling mud pools which noisily burble, gurgle and splutter everywhere.

From the park I drove to Golden Springs and hired a rather basic cabin in secluded camp site in the woods on road to Napier. It's very picturesque with its own thermal pools. I managed to use two of them but was slightly put off by the dark brownish water and slippery steps. And then it started to rain again! So ate inside my rather isolated cabin, making a tortilla with onion, potato, garlic, tomato and oregano bought in Rotorua, washed down with the white wine Rosemarie had given me. The cabin is set amongst tall looming pines and I could hear constant tapping noises. Slightly scary. Didn't sleep well and was plagued by annoying sand flies the whole night! When I woke I was bitten all down my right arm which started to swell up. My driving arm as well! Had an odd dream and woke up saying:

'A dog ran wild…'! No idea why. Am I a dog running wild? Don't think so. I like to be in control, even when running. I can't imagine running wild, diving off the rocks into treacherous sea or getting abominably drunk… I like my 'aloneness', my musings, the wonders of nature, reading and writing this journal… Found account of Katherine Mansfield's 1907 trip to Tikitere (Hell's Gate) in Rotorua, a sacred place associated with the Ngati Rangiteaorere tribe and only thermal park still Maori-owned.

On a whim, am experimenting with acrostic poems on all the places I'm visiting and have gone back to beginning to add them all:

NAPIER (*Ahuriri* in Māori)
No nihilism,
Apathy or atheism.
Pantheism perhaps
Is always an
Everlasting
Reward.

Napier is the famous Art-Deco town with an abundance of pretty purple Jacaranda trees. It was rebuilt after the 1931 earthquake which killed 256 people. Apparently 4000 hectares of Napier was under the sea until the earthquake raised them up. Came here via Hastings but didn't go straight into town but turned off coast road to find Bayview camp site, listed in book. Given lovely cabin with fridge, small cooker, electric kettle, toaster and great hot shower – at great price. Did laundry then drove into Napier for cheap beer, tacos and dips. Got back and cooked breast of chicken and garlic in a little white wine, served with boiled potatoes and avocado salad. Drank remaining white wine and felt happy! I'm turning into an 'alkie'! Camp site's very sheltered and covered in awnings so ate outside in communal dining area even though it looked like rain. Chatted to a few people then retired to cabin and slept like the proverbial log. However remembered one dream: *My body's disintegrating; my skin, muscles, organs are vanishing and I'm only a skeleton – with rustling, creaking bones. Like a marionette (reminiscent of the wooden horses in the play 'Warhorse') I have to be manipulated but I manage to rise up. It's dark but the full moon's shining. I venture out and hundreds of skeletons dance in a circle round and round. I try to join them but they glide away amongst the moonlit trees. Two or three remain. I reach out to them but they collapse and crumble into dust...*

This morning bought green-stone pendant from camp site owner. He said it was bad luck to keep umbrella open inside (?).

WELLINGTON – *Katherine Mansfield's birthplace*
Well, all is well,
Ending what is
Low
Level
Insipidity.
No dirt or
Grime in this
Town.
On to the
New, now...

It's finally stopped raining! Arrived in Wellington late so treated myself to a hotel on Route 1. Checked in and got bus into town; had gin and tonic in trendy over-priced bar then a very good inexpensive meal at tiny Vietnamese place, where I chatted to the girls at counter overlooking kitchen. Got bus back and slept well but awoke early to more rain.

After breakfast I drove jeep and parked near the Te Papa museum; bought fish called 'Tarakihi' in harbour market.

Jotted down KM's quote: 'Wellington is a small town planted at the edge of a fine deep harbour, like a lake. Behind it on either side there are hills. The houses are built of light painted wood. They have iron roofs coloured red. And there're big dark plumy trees, massed together… '*Daphne*'. 1921.

The Te Papa Tongarewa is New Zealand's national museum and art gallery. Papa Tongarewa roughly means 'the place of treasures of this land'. It contains many diverse and multidisciplinary collections but I didn't see anything I particularly liked. Australian aborigine paintings are much more fascinating and beautiful but on the other hand, Maoris seem to have a much better life in New Zealand than the Aborigines in Australia (although there were tensions in colonial society as KM sensitively mentions). Maoris are adept at keeping their culture alive in an entrepreneurial sense but Aboriginals, apart from their fantastic paintings, unscrupulously exploited, have no national voice and no true sense of self. Somebody explained this to me as being a geographical problem. New Zealand is relatively small and communications between North Island and South Island are good whereas Australia is a vast continent and Aborigine tribes live in isolation without a common language or identity.

Visited Katherine Mansfield House Museum. Parked near the Parliament (parking pretty easy in NZ). It was so windy I could scarcely close the car door. I headed to Tinakori Road in Thorndon, home to many artists. It was difficult to see any numbers and I worried I wouldn't find way back but eventually I found the right house – no. 25 – but it was 4pm and shut! And suddenly I felt exhausted – overcome with fatigue. Went back to hotel and had a rest then carried on reading the KM journal ... heard loud banging noises, odd as the hotel seemed so quiet before.

Left early morning but ferry across Cook Strait to Picton was delayed so I bought a little dress for Delphine and had tea on the harbour front. Wrote some post cards then drove on to ferry. My money's diminishing fast. Oh well... The crossing was very calm and in blazing sunshine! I stayed on deck and surveyed the scenery even though my arms and face got burnt. Unaccustomed to this rare sun and can't stop sneezing...

PICTON
Poised on the bay
In Marlborough Sound.
Carefully tended, yet no cutesy
Town – just tidily compact.
Off from the ferry crossing –
North Island to South Island.

After we landed, had a quick walk around Picton, at the head of Queen Charlotte Sound and on north-east of South Island. Apparently it's named after Sir Thomas Picton, the Duke of Wellington's military associate killed at the Battle of Waterloo. KM spent time in Picton where her paternal grandparents and father lived after arriving from Australia. She refers to it in '*The Voyage*', describing the ferry ride from Wellington by a woman taking her grandchild to Picton after the child's mother, her daughter, had sadly died.

Tuesday
BLEINHEIM – *tried a short run but had to give up!*
Bountiful, wine country in
Lowlands of the coastal plain
Engaging the palate, amusing
Nosegays; full fruitiness; acute aromas.

Here, there and everywhere
Enough vineyards to fill a whole country
In the vastness of the prairie
Marlborough Sounds …good…

In Blenheim (In Māori: Waiharakeke = 'The waters of Flax') after a coastal route detour, going up part of Queen Charlotte Sound. It's the biggest town in Marlborough wine region and on the confluence of two rivers. This is a tectonically active area with several small earthquakes each year so hopefully there won't be one while I'm here! It's supposed to have the sunniest climate, with hot, dry summers and crisp winters. Not particularly hot when I arrived but at least it wasn't raining! Staying in hostel accommodation and it rained throughout the night (I was tossing and turning!) and was still wet this morning so I went to Cloudy Bay winery. I tasted five different wines including a red Pinot Noir and a sweet Gewürztraminer dessert wine which was a one-off (botrytis-affected) last year. Bought a bottle for Adam. It's only 50 ml. so should fit snugly into my suitcase, wrapped in a smelly sock! Returned to hostel and cooked some lunch in communal kitchen and chatted to some German boys and a Russian girl. In the afternoon visited another small vineyard recommended by Arnold, the hostel owner. He's married to a Chinese girl called Chile, nearly 20 years younger than him. He was interested in my French name and said I looked like Diane Keaton! Then he asked why my umbrella was up when it wasn't raining (!). Walked into town and back then made quick pasta with tomatoes. I knocked back an entire bottle of Sauvignon Blanc 'Clean Skins', an overproduced wine distributed without a label, but not bad. Felt mellow and relaxed and slept until 6am.

I'm made of wood –
Solid cuts of teak form my articulated,

Clumsy limbs and stubborn torso.
I can sit and stand,
Bend my knees and arms
And nod my head.
To make movements
I must be pressed.
Then I collapse.

Had breakfast outside as sun was shining! Then it became cloudy with a cold wind blowing in from Cook Strait. Drove to bakery, went to market across the way and bought very cheap green-stone pendant and cherry jam.

Thursday – *can't find my umbrella!*
NELSON
Nelson, home to new boy settlers
Educating Rita Angus at Cass.
Long walk to waterfront and
Spectacular Boat Shed Café.
Overpriced but tasty food.
Nelson, large, expansive, settlers settled now…

Nelson in Māori is Whakatū = 'build' or 'establish'. It's on eastern shore of Tasman Bay, the most important and oldest city in South Island. Many roads are named after people and ships connected to Nelson; Trafalgar Street being the main shopping area of the city. Inhabitants are referred to as 'Nelsonians'.

There were several camp sites listed and eventually found one I thought was nearest the town. Walked miles from there to the waterfront and had drinks and tapas at one place before treating myself to a meal at the Boatshed restaurant Adam insisted I visit. Beautiful setting on pier overlooking bay but crayfish I ordered was so tiny I was given a reduction so treated myself to fab *pannacotta* with baked apricots and blueberries, all washed down with bottle of local Sauvignon. Waitresses were rather sniffy but one Maori girl was very pleased with tip I left. Returned to tapas bar and chap called taxi for me. In bed by 10pm and awake at 5am and have developed terrible cough. Just finished reading Katherine Mansfield's journal. I was willing her not to die. Feeling confused and upset now...

Had breakfast, ironed and packed everything, including umbrella. This incessant rain has affected me badly. Feel okay when sun's out but overcast again today. Expected rain but didn't think it would be as relentless as this. Continuous downpour to Havelock, the world capital of green mussels, where I stopped for lunch and devoured some very meaty mussels, served with garlic and soda bread. There was a poetry reading in café which I very much enjoyed. Poems by Zarah Butcher; Linda Connell and Anne French but Fleur Adcock was quoted. I've always loved her name:

Fleur de lys, Fleur de lit, Fleur de sel
Fleur de sea, Flower girl.
Ad hoc flower to cock
Cock to flower, cock to flour
Cock flowers, cook flour
Add flower – flour flowers
Fleurgette flowers, cock-gette flowers
Fleur d'amie
Cooked in flour and love...

ABEL TASMAN PARK – *can't remember getting here!*

Abel Tasman National Park divides the Golden and Tasman Bays and is over 50 km. long. It's named after Abel Tasman, a Dutch explorer who sighted New Zealand in 1642. There was hardly anyone on the huge stretch of beach even though this coast track's very popular. Lots of kayaking opportunities but I didn't quite feel up to that! Saw many herons and oyster catchers. The vivid contrast of the corn-yellow sand, deep green forest, dazzling blue seas, pools and skies had a bewitching beauty. I love the specially constructed pathways and designated walks such as here: all in a variety of distances or levels of difficulty. It makes it easier to decide what I can manage. Took the two-mile walking track to Porter's Beach. (Haven't really run since my op. but regular exercise does reduce fatigue. Walking every day in Nettlebury did make me feel more energetic.) The walk in the national park was lovely and I wasn't too tired at the end.

Saturday? – *Took long route by mistake…*
MURCHISON
Misty no more.
Underlying the greenest of green
Rivers yet
Clear with a clean clarity
Holy waters ebbing and flowing
In the
Spring
Of miraculous
Nadir

Been away over a week now and not sure what day it is! Phoned Adam who sounded worried about me but assured him I was fine, regardless of my husky voice and cough! Have beautiful cabin on outskirts of Murchison, which seems like a one-horse town at the confluence of the Buller and Matakitaki Rivers. Historically it was teeming with gold miners and early settlers.

Arrived early so walked into town for a beer and shopping. Got back to cabin and made pasta with asparagus, plus lettuce and avocado salad, washed down with tumblers of New Zealand Shiraz. Added ice as it was rather lukewarm … My throat and chest very painful so didn't eat much but wine did me good… Had a bottle of Mystic Peak, a Sauvignon Blanc from the Waihopai Valley I picked up on my travels … *drunk, sick woman tumbles off rocks…* felt extremely sleepy so went to bed very early – a mistake. Woke up at 4am thinking there was someone in the room as there was so much rattling going on; then I thought a nasty rodent or reptile had crept in. Suddenly realised it could be earthquake tremors. There were strong shock-waves for only about 20 seconds, but remember thinking: *well if it's the end, so be it!* …Reading 'Any Human Heart' by William Boyd which I've nearly finished! He discusses death and luck and to have drawn out death would be bad luck. Hope my death isn't drawn out. I want to die instantaneously, with assistance, if necessary; that's why I've drawn up my living will, but stupidly it's in England – it should be here with me… Forgot to ask people about tremors but no one seemed bothered… My hair's a wild, tangled mess. Can't be bothered to wash it and anyway I've lost my shampoo.

PUNAKAIKI *– I am grasping the 'cold knob' of my umbrella; as if to reality*

Perceived pancake formations
Under the crumbling
Network of rocks
And all things
Kiwi in this manifestation.
An
Inviting, intriguing
Key to it displayed
Inside my head.

Headed along the coast to Punakaiki, on edge of Paparoa National Park and famous for the '*Pancake Rocks*' at Dolomite Point. The rocks are heavily eroded limestone and the sea bursts through the vertical blow holes during high tides. There's a constructed walkway around the coastal rocks to view every aspect of the intricately shaped volcanic rock formations, slowly being washed away by the sea.

I walked around most of the rocks and was struck by the magic of nature in these wonderful formations. Waves of sadness rushed over me. I felt so alone… For some reason Virginia Woolf putting rocks in her pockets and drowning herself in the River Ouse during World War Two came to mind. Not sure why… I'm using my umbrella as a walking stick…

My thoughts and feelings are confused.
Is death coming? Is my cancer inevitably fatal?

Feeling ill but comforted by merino polo neck sweater bought in Nelson. I'm wearing four layers of clothing plus cagoule as my bones are so icy. After visiting the rocks I drove to Westport and then inland along the bewitching, emerald green opacity (like crème de menthe) of River Buller. New Zealand has so much empty space, so few inhabitants and so many mysteries…

In between clouds of despondency, I feel ripples of exhilaration…

Monks House, Rodmell.
Fast moving clouds casting shadows over the velvet green downs.

Long walk to the river edge, rocks in pockets, at high tide
Dragging you downstream to Asham Wharf.

Flora and Fauna I've seen in New Zealand:
Main flora: lupins; foxgloves; New Zealand flax (like spiky blood-red gladiola; many species of roses and types of

fuchsia. Lupins grow like weeds on South Island along main roads and streams in exquisite hues of reds, oranges, pinks… Strangest thing I've seen is a Leopard Seal on beach near here. At first I thought it was dead but it was stretched out, resting. Met national park ranger who said they were horrible, ugly creatures who swallow rocks so that they can grind up shellfish. Like their namesake, they're the fiercest and most formidable hunters of all seals, seeking warm-bloodied prey, even other seals. Saw some 'wekas': sturdy brown flightless birds about the size of a chicken. Haven't seen any kiwis! They're now quite rare and are kept live in special museums. However lots of sheep, goats, cows, horses, deer and alpacas, which at first I thought were llamas. Also saw some large chaffinch-like birds and some exotic seagulls.

I spy the albatross,
Make a grab at it
And clasp my arms around its neck.
It pulls me under the cold sea; an ice sheet.
Spluttering, coughing I struggle to keep afloat.
The albatross around my neck.

I've been staring at the sea for hours. Ever-changing, dramatic, violent, noisy, crashing waves lapping at vanishing rocks, swallowing them whole, so enticing… I could easily step in and disappear… no one would ever know… but what about AA?

An observation:

Throughout South Island I've encountered many non-automated single lane level crossings. And sometimes the railway line goes through the middle of a roundabout! It's very difficult to see any oncoming traffic or trains. I looked them up on the hostel computer in Blenheim as I was curious to find out more about them. There're nearly 1400, fewer than half protected by flashing red lights and bells and only a quarter with added half-arm barriers. The rest are only controlled by 'Stop and Give Way' signs which I find extremely worrying. Apparently many accidents and deaths have occurred over the last few years; would be even worse if traffic volume was greater. There are measures to make them safer, especially since the sister of a famous cricketer, Chris something, was killed in an accident. I recall a single-lane bridge with walled-sides over the river, north of Hokitika, where vehicles and trains shared the same track! I found this really frightening because as well as giving way to oncoming traffic, I had to make sure there was no train coming before I started to cross the bridge. It was also disconcerting to drive over the bumpy raised railway track and very difficult to see ahead. I confess that, on one occasion, I took pot luck, hoping there was no oncoming vehicle! The crossings appear quite suddenly and I bet other drivers, not just me, are taking risks. A serendipitous way to die perhaps, with train looming towards you. Unfortunately very inconvenient for train driver and passengers...

Sunday? – *feeling strange, fragile, broken...*
HOKITIKA
Holy holy holy!
Old gold miners putting
Kettles on fires
In the sandy lowlands.
Telling tales of adventures to
Inquiring, inquisitive listeners.
Killing time
Again and again.

Hokitika ('place of return') is about 25 miles south of Greymouth, close to the mouth of the Hokitika River. It was part of the West Coast Gold Rush. I could see Mount Cook

(Aoraki) from its main street. Hokitika's famous for green-stone but it was very expensive compared to before so didn't buy any more.

I see a massive rock face of dark grey limestone. On it is an enormous pale grey-green ring drawn in chalk. As I get closer it looks hairy or as if it is made of iron filings, almost alive, like millions of caterpillars walking around a giant circle. Then I find a rat, quivering, in the last throes of death, like my shaky handwriting, now almost unintelligible...

It was very late by the time I arrived at camp-site via Greymouth and it's still pouring with rain but managed to get a standard cabin. Very few people staying in camp-sites and I've never had trouble finding accommodation for the night. Woman owner advised me to drive straight to town before restaurants shut and recommended a fish one. I had catch of the day – fish fried in batter – with far too many chips; only ate a quarter of it – *and* it was described as a light dish. I'm losing my appetite. A Kiwi chappie chatted me up! – said I was French and couldn't understand! *No sex, please, well past my sell-by-date!* When I drove back it was still raining very hard. Driving in this perpetual, persistent rain is killing my soul and the final straw was when I got out of the jeep floods of water poured onto me from broken guttering on parking bay roof. I was soaking wet *and* I broke umbrella so was relieved to climb into cabin to get dry. Was so exhausted went straight to bed. Slept for a long time as I took two of the anti-histamine pills I had for my bites. They were stronger than sleeping pills and I slept 11 hours until 8.30am! Maybe I could just take the rest of them if everything gets too much … Dreamt of crowds waving red flax at Passion procession with Father Gabriel as Christ figure beating himself with it! Showered and made breakfast and then headed back to town. Not feeling great and my chesty cough's worse. It was still raining; foggy grey and bloody cold! To cheer myself up bought a turquoise merino/possum shawl similar to the one Adam sent me which, stupidly, I didn't think I would need! I wrapped it around myself straight away. Flustered woman in shop gave me strange look, announcing abruptly she didn't really believe in recession until recently. The Greymouth mining disaster did affect the mood of the locals and they've just stopped buying now. She also said that New Zealand mines had a terrible health and safety record. She was fanning herself as if she was hot (but I was cold!) and said she'd only bought the business in May, so very concerned. I filled up at BP station. Petrol nearly half the price compared to Europe so pleased at least one thing's cheaper here. Went back to cabin and packed up. Hope I haven't forgotten anything this time.

Monday?

Managed to get lost driving out of Hokitika. Went round and round in circles but eventually found right road and drove through the most marvellous scenery to Arthur's Pass. The landscape dramatically changes shape and colour: greens, greys and yellows and clusters of red, purple and pink lupin flowers everywhere with the majestic 'Castle Rocks' sweeping up into pointed peaks beyond mossy, rounded hillocks. Possibly the best scenery I've ever seen. Not many towns on this long, straight road so went across country to Littleton from where I'll head to Christchurch. Feeling more hopeful again. Maybe I don't want to die after all. When I get back to England, I will phone Dr Chandra…

Think I am running out of in…

*

This journal was discovered at Copthorne Hotel, Christchurch Central, in the aftermath of the city's earthquake. The hotel suffered no serious casualties.

*

Loose page:

Am I going mad?
Am I going bad?
Behaving erratically...
Thank Christ
It's not Oxford.
The Church of Christ
Christ's church,
Christ's mass.
No chew
Chew train
Chugging down
The track.
No being stoned
For driving
In Saudi.
No one
On my back.
No rock tautology
Only seismology
Here in
Ōtautahi.
Hi!

ND - #0280 - 270225 - C0 - 216/138/14 - PB - 9780993010668 - Matt Lamination